ALEX DRAKE
and
FRIENDS

ALEX DRAKE and FRIENDS

The Lost Cabin

AADITYA RAJ

Vitasta

To my readers,

You are the best :)

Published by
Renu Kaul Verma
Vitasta Publishing Pvt Ltd
4348/4C, Ansari Road, Daryaganj
New Delhi - 110 002
info@vitastapublishing.com

ISBN: 978-81-963329-9-0

First Edition 2024
MRP ₹350

This novel is entirely a work of fiction. Names, characters, events and incidents are entirely imaginary. Reference to real places, actual regions, institutions or community practices has been made in a fictitious manner. Any resemblance to actual persons, living or dead or actual events is purely coincidental.

Edited by Ridhima Gandhi
Typeset & Cover Design by Somesh Kumar Mishra
Printed by Vikas Computer and Printers, New Delhi

Contents

Intro: A few words from the Author... ix

Chapter 1 Dimension Two 1

Chapter 2 A Reckless Bargain 15

Chapter 3 Liquechloro Liquefies 28

Chapter 4 Alexander the Great 41

Chapter 5 A *Lovely* Little Excursion to *Friendly* Outer Space 62

Chapter 6 Sternind Institute of Realm Power learning 79

Chapter 7 Why do concepts have to be so Complicated? 102

Chapter 8 Peter Colter 143

Chapter 9 Pressure is Pressurizing 160

Chapter 10	In for Goosebumps	171
Chapter 11	Gotta find him quick…	192
Chapter 12	Well, we've gotten into bit of a situation here…	199
Chapter 13	This was not supposed to happen, was it?	218
Chapter 14	The Lost Cabin	233
Chapter 15	Revelations	239

Intro
A few words from the Author...

Okay, so... There wasn't really supposed to be an "Intro," you know. But I figured that some of you might be having little idea about what certain references in this book indicate. That's why I'm here, preventing you from heading straight to the first chapter with this stupid intervention. What I think worth mentioning is... Well, I wrote another book earlier, titled *Alex Drake and friends : Wasor Island*, which if you haven't read, you need not bother about right now. You know, I think of *Wasor Island* as more of a prequel to this book than the other way round. So, here's a quick recap of important events in Alex Drake's world. (*Who is Alex Drake?* Yeah, we're gonna cover that too) So let's get started.

We'll see the world through the eyes of Alex Drake, a young man of twenty-two (I think I would've called him "smart" too, but guess I'll just leave that for you to figure out yourself). He has sharp, deep-set eyes, along with an attractive face. He's a rich-but-not-spoiled guy, who manages a part of his huge family business and lives with his parents in the same locality as his childhood friends—Lester and Angelina.

Lester – Alex's best friend – is quite wild but fun to be around. He is tall but not much of a fitness freak (yeah you can say that by looking at the little protruding belly he has), with long spiky hair and a large crooked nose (He sometimes looks crazy with his outfit. Like, straight up bonkers. Other than that, he's cool). At the age of twenty, he has had enough life experiences to be able to tackle problems under immense pressure.

Angelina – She's half the definition of a beautiful eighteen-year-old and half the definition of a weirdly intriguing young woman. She has pea-green eyes, with long and thick, wavy brown hair. But don't let that fool you. She *can* sometimes act like an annoying little kid.

So, to get you caught up on the events until Chapter One of this book, let me brief you on the story *of Alex Drake and friends : Wasor Island.*

Alex, along with his friends, agrees to go on a leisure trip to Japan. But their journey is interrupted abruptly. After safely landing on water – in the middle of nowhere – they decide to take refuge on a nearby island. It seems only like a weird deserted island at first, until a horde of anomalously peculiar animals starts chasing them. As they successfully escape from these animals, they come across an old and ruined mansion where a strange old man named Vishwaroopaha (also called Mr V) discloses the story of the curse that was inflicted upon the island along with the way to its cure—A series of ten deadly challenges.

Yeah, sorry if I'm going a bit too fast. It *is* a novel, after all.

After analysing their options for a while, they embark on the quest to cure the island, in order to be able to survive until help arrives.

>>Fast forward to the end of the fourth challenge>>

Due to a massive volcano explosion (Yeah. *Volcano Explosion*. Not Volcanic Eruption. Just bear with it), Angelina is separated from Alex and Lester.

>>Fast forward again to the ninth challenge>>

Alex reunites with Angelina, and they continue with their tasks. Meanwhile, Lester being "quite occupied at the moment" (*cough cough* captured and put in chains *cough cough*). As the tenth challenge begins, Angelina turns into a demon, which Alex assumes as a part of the task.

>>Fast forward yet again to their success in the mission>>

They return to Florida after being rescued from the island. Unexpectedly, Alex's Uncle Edward arrives out of nowhere and decides to stay with them and spends a few days with him and his friends. One night before going to bed, Uncle Edward approaches Alex and intriguingly says, 'Remember me?'

After much rumination, Alex realizes that Uncle Edward is Vishwaroopaha, the same old man on the island who had revealed information regarding the curse. Vishwaroopaha explains that he's a "man with a bit of occult" sent by Wasor Island's magic, to help Alex in his life. Well, that still remains a question—Is he?

So, there you go. I guess now you're all prepped to start reading. Go on, then. I won't interrupt you.

Chapter 1

Dimension Two

Dawn cracked the sky with faint streaks of orange. As if some force was trying to convey the presence of the sun to him, Alex woke up… while he was still sleeping—He just *knew* that he was dreaming because, honestly, no man in an all-blue outfit and a brown hat, holding a book labelled GUIDE close to his chest could've appeared standing in the burning campfire visible through his room window. 'Wasor is still giving me nightmares, but nowadays, friendly ones like this man... Doesn't let me catch at least a little bit of sleep peacefully...' he thought as he turned over on the bed facing the other side, all the while finalizing his interpretations of that man's character.

After uncle Edward revealed his true identity, Alex began to experience horrific nightmares, some even more intense than the challenges he faced back at Wasor. Back home, when he had asked Vishwaroopaha – the one and only man who had disguised himself as Alex's uncle – where his *real* uncle was, Vishwaroopaha had replied in an uncanny tone, 'Your uncle... Um, he passed away five years ago.'

Although Alex was shook by this news, he was incapable of conveying it to his parents, who hadn't heard from uncle Edward since the last seven years. Uncle Edward used to keep himself isolated from the rest of the family. But, when he *was* with them, he was a fun guy. Alex guessed that maybe this was the reason their family didn't mind him not being in touch.

The only people amongst whom did this information about the real Uncle Edward circulate were Lester, Alex and Angelina.

The days had passed smoothly, until Alex saw this thin man smiling, in what he *thought of* as his dream. Suddenly Vishwaroopaha, along with Lester and Angelina entered the room. Without giving so much as a glance to Alex, Vishwaroopaha engaged himself in a deep conversation with the man through the window, while Alex's two friends scooted over to him.

'Why is this dream too detailed and long?' Alex asked Lester as he got out of his blanket and sat up straight.

'Well, putting it into complex words... I guess your misunderstanding and suspicions are obvious. I thought that this night was a dream too, but when Mr V solidified out of thin air in my bedroom, waking me up with a blast of bright yellow light, I ruled out the doubt that this wasn't real. Dude, it scared the ghost outta me. He was like, "Yeah, I have *sensed your uneasiness* and blah blah blah, but I'm *afraid* that part of this is just for a little petty wish"...' Lester replied in an exaggerating but unsure tone when Vishwaroopaha asked them to gather around, announcing, 'Come on over, you three. There's no time to fuss around. We need to hurry. There's something to be discussed...'

'So,' he exclaimed reasonably. 'This is all by fate, to fate and *for* fate. The three of you have to head to a realm. This way, we'll all be set for the future and that petty wish of yours shall be fulfilled, Alex. It was truly a foolish wish. You know how we start blabbering anything when we're stressed? Though all that stuff we say is vague, but it's actually our heart's core desire—our heart's *main wish* at that point of time. Well, anyway, you know, I take everything seriously, being the kind of understanding gentleman I am. So, I've...' he gave a slight chuckle that faltered momentarily.

'But all in all, Alex, you'll know what your wish was and how that is to be fulfilled at the right time. All you need to know now though, is what I said back at Wasor: **Surroundings are going to be deceptive**. They're still so, boy. The chapter hasn't ended. You've just started...' Vishwaroopaha continued.

'Started what... Getting a headache...?' Alex thought as he wrestled with a burning feeling in his throat, which he for sure knew was nervousness, not that hot ball of air in his body while he was getting through the seventh challenge at Wasor Island. The fact that Alex was being addressed by Vishwaroopaha on a serious matter rattled him. He feared the very thought that it may lead to something like those challenges.

Vishwaroopaha turned his attention to that man as suddenly as he had left a deep imprint on Alex's mind by saying those words rapidly. He asked the man, '*Nerdhlic hagcne*, okay, Mr Brown?'

'Yes sir,' the man replied—It all wasn't Alex's hallucination, after all. He was a thin, skinny man with a very short, almost faded moustache and pretty long legs. His hair was parted like a curtain. Alex wondered if that man had some biological problem in his legs or if he'd worked as a clown in a circus earlier.

'Now, all three of you are bound to luck. Of course, everyone is, but I feel that you three are special. That's why I've decided to get you all to Sternind. Mr Droller Brown will be your guide for the day. He'll tell what you are in for,' said Vishwaroopaha. 'Just step into the burning campfire outside, and don't worry, the fire is harmless for now. Off you go. All queries are to be answered on the way.'

He again turned towards Mr Brown and said, 'All planned? Everything...? None of the Sternindians should see them in this condition, okay?'

Alex wanted to spring out of his bed to ask him what was wrong with their condition, but he decided against it. After all, he was in his night suit, a grey shirt and pyjamas. Lester wore his night suit, which was covered with green stripes that stood out on the yellow fabric.

Angelina looked dressed in party wear; 'Dang, maybe she's been yanked out of some party just for this,' Alex thought.

But Angelina didn't seem angry or upset about missing the party, rather she looked interested whenever Vishwaroopaha mentioned "fate" or "Realm".

'Wait,' Alex said. 'Where are we going, and why should we trust *you*? Who's this guy, and how can we just go blindly without informing anyone?'

Vishwaroopaha turned towards him, with a firm look in his eyes. 'Well, for now, Alex, I want you to consider this as a threat and an obligation.'

'Wha–'

'Now, before you try to resist,' Vishwaroopaha said, moving his fingers in a certain pattern, 'I need to show you a fraction of what I can, and will do if you don't yield.'

A sense of horror took over Alex. Before he could realize what was going on, he had risen up in the air, and been thrown out of the window by an invisible force that left the glass pane shattered. He felt a sharp pain in his hands and face, as glass pieces wedged their way through his skin. No one reacted. They just stood inside the house, not even blinking. It seemed like the world had paused, stopped moving. Risking a quick look through the broken window as he flew uncontrolled, Alex noticed Vishwaroopaha smiling.

He was lying right next to the campfire in the front lawn. He tried standing up, but found himself levitating again, and feeling as if his arms and legs were out of his control. Once again, he was drifted into the air with great speed and was just about to be rammed head-first into a brick wall, when he immediately stopped. The invisible force gripped him again and dragged him to where he was standing before all of this had happened. The window repaired itself in front of Alex's eyes, and he found himself healing while glass worked its way out of his skin. Before everyone started moving again, Vishwaroopaha said sternly, 'I could've made this a lot worse.'

Great. The last thing Alex need in his life was a personal ass-whupping by Vishwaroopaha. Guess he *did* have his fair share of experiences in life.

Lester spoke up, 'Yeah, Alex is right. Where are we going, and why should we trust you?'

'Um…' Alex said before Vishwaroopaha had a chance to say anything, 'On second thought, I think we *can* trust him, Lester. I guess this time you can blame me if anything goes wrong.'

'But– You know what… Whatever. Fine,' Lester said, raising his hands in a quick surrendering gesture.

'In fact, I assure you…' Vishwaroopaha started talking about "implementation of safety protocols" and how "trust is something that is achieved with time".

Lester whispered to Alex, 'When are his lectures gonna get over? I'm feeling... Bad. And nervous. And shocked. And... Well, are we gonna get into a tunnel or something? What's this *Sternind*?' His voice was loud enough for Angelina to overhear it. Before Alex could get a chance to formulate a reply, Angelina said, 'Guess what– I'm not nervous, horrified or whatever *at all.* I'm… intrigued. Let's see what this is...' Angelina said, putting *nervous* and *horrified* in air quotes.

'Good luck Alex, Lester and Angelina. I'll meet you all again, at... Um... A very unexpected moment. And, by the way, don't worry about your parents and your presence here, at your home. You might not be at home, but to them, you'll be at home,' Vishwaroopaha said, just as he produced three smartphones from his coat pocket and handed them to Alex and his friends as they set foot into the campfire after heading outside into the main lawn.

To Alex, the flames didn't feel hot, rather cool, *soothing* cool. They were effectively getting all the tiredness of the previous day – when Alex and Lester had participated in a Half Marathon event – out of Alex's legs.

With reference to the mobile phones, Alex questioned Vishwaroopaha, 'Mobile Phones… What are these for…? I didn't quite understand what you said...'

'Oh, these aren't phones. They're devices that'll control your clone. Yes, you heard right. A clone of yours will be created once you leave this place, and these *Control Yourself* devices shall be activated. Just use them as a single-player game. What you do with your model in those CY devices, will also happen in real life, at your home. You can type messages for what you have to say, regardless of the time taken to write them. It'll all be done in a jiffy. You'll see your home and the live actions of all the people here, in perfect 4K resolution. You'll perform the entire day's activities, and see everything that happens during that time—in just an hour. The clone and its actions are not just for your residence, but for the whole Earth. Because you're getting to go somewhere that is not on Earth... Anyway, be grateful you're even chosen to be there, amongst them. Good luck again,' replied Vishwaroopaha, again in a long lecture-like manner.

'You mean we'll see the whole day in just an hour? We'll see the future with those devices? Can that be changed... Or not...? What *is* it? How can we possibly fiddle with time...?' Alex objected.

Vishwaroopaha smiled. 'It *will* be a whole day, but in Sternind, it'll just feel like an hour. Even the effect of the digital screen on your eyes will just be like an hour of Earth.'

Just as he said so, Alex's room dissolved into nothingness, as if pixel-by-pixel of vision. Alex found himself and his friends with Mr Brown flying through the skies, on *surfing boards*...?

'I've heard of surfing on waves, surfing on the web, but surfing in the air, wow, *that's* just cool. Surfing on the not-so-high waves at the beach really pays off, man,' Alex thought. He was just... Amazed.

The sun had started to rise a little. And there they were, surfing through the air in multi-coloured surfboards.

But this series of sudden strange moments didn't appeal to his common sense much. 'Who are "they"? What is *Nerdhlic Hagcne*? What is "Sternind"?' A bunch of unending questions filled his mind.

The answer seemed to be… Mr Droller Brown. So as soon as the opportunity presented itself, Alex banked to the right while air-surfing, closer to Mr Brown's surf, enjoying the air whizzing past him. But Angelina was faster. 'Mr Brown, could you please let us know what are we "*in for*," as Mr Vishwaroopaha had assured us information?'

Mr Brown replied in a confused tone but straightened his attitude later, 'Vishwa...? Er– I mean... Well, you know, or… I bet you *don't* know, the explanation of what we're in for is pretty complicated. So, it starts with a few things you need to firmly understand. See, contrary to the common belief that the Earth is one as a whole, there are three spheres of the same planet. It is the same planet existing at the same place, but the realms, which I previously called the spheres—Also known as the *dimensions* of the same planet make all the difference. This, which you call "Earth," is actually not a planet. Truly, it's only one dimension of this planet, out of three. I know it's hard for you to believe this, but it *is* the reality. Now you might be thinking of what I'm referring to as "this planet". Doesn't it have a name? Well, this planet possesses some kind of anomalous power, which enables it to create another dimension of itself as soon as you give a name to it. This indicates that nothing is greater than this planet around us, in our solar system. When you named it "Earth," another dimension popped up. So we have the second Realm, Sternind. But since it also has been given a name, the third dimension has been created, whose name is not widely accepted considering that very few people actually know it. So we have three dimensions. "Well," you might say, "what's the harm in making infinite dimensions like this?" And the answer to that is that whenever one gives a name to a new dimension and it starts being commonly spoken by many, another dimension is created. But, the inventor of the name is cursed to stay there forever and face the dangers of the place all by himself, with no help and no way to escape. These dimensions are more or less just like Earth, having water, oxygen and an atmosphere. But the landforms are totally different. There are new minerals, ores, wind patterns and most importantly, people in a new habitat adapted to a different way of a living. And I'll explain about them in a little bit. You understood whatever I said?'

'So, you mean to say, that no one dares to name the third Realm and make it official now, because if he does so, he will be cursed to remain confined to the place forever?'

'You got it right.'

'Hold on a minute–' Lester said, 'What do you mean by "the dangers there"?'

'Well, the native creatures, which I don't need to elaborate about,' Mr Brown replied, but after seeing Lester's sheepish expression continued, 'They're actually more like animals– Well, no. "Animals" is quite a sober term for them. Considering what the founder of Sternind encountered first… Guess he was just lucky to have been able to get the word out about the second Realm,' Mr Brown paused for a moment, with a *lost-deep-in-thoughts* expression on his face.

He continued, 'Anyway, there are three dimensions—Three spheres, as I said. The first one is known as Earth, where you are from. The second one is known as Sternind and it's a long story how this realm – the realm we are heading to – *our* realm, Sternind was named. But we better not start about its past right now. All I can say is that the people living in Sternind are called the Sternindians. Not *stern Indians*, mind you. Sternind's residents are not limited to just stern Indians, though you *can* find some of them there, indeed. People from any corner of Earth and Sternind can rightfully be in Sternind, but not until they know how to make use of RP or are learning it. Oh and before you start with questions again, I'll just say that we'll get to the term "RP" later. Anyway, the name Sternind is coined from the two terms, *western* and ***India***. It's just because the "western" people investigated and found out about the concept of Realms in India. India is actually the root of the matter. It so happened, that the wester… Uh? Ugh… I was saying we must not ponder over Sternind's history right now, but my mouth just doesn't shut up. Anyway, let's get back to the three realms… The third realm was created due to a mistake the Sternindians had committed, before they truly understood the concept of the realms. They had named the second dimension "Sternind" and that's why the third dimension evolved—Okay, I can't believe I'm talking about *that* one, but, it seems there is a need for you all to learn about it. The third realm, most deadly and dangerous of them all, is named... I'd better not say it out loud. Why would I, anyway? We don't want a fourth realm to be created, do we? Just saying the word dispels high frequency terror waves, much more intense than your silly atom bombs. That is the realm under the dictatorship of a man popularly known as the "Savage Person", whose intentions are pretty destructive but clear... Anyway, I reckon you must not try to get there, even if–' Mr Brown suddenly paused for a moment, with a look on his face like a student has when he reaches school unprepared, only to be reminded that he has his final examination that day. He reached for his pocket, trying to take something out.

Subsequently, there was abrupt silence for a short while, except for the sound of air rushing past them. As Alex looked down at the grassy meadows which resembled plain green paper speckled with a tinge of brown, he wondered what must be going on with Lester—He was acrophobic. As Alex looked over at his direction, he seemed fine. Maybe Lester's surf was magical, or he had finally overcome his fear, or maybe he was just lost in deep thought about Mr Brown's startling words. All those facts had rattled Alex; they were hard for him to take in. He decided to leave the matter as it was, believing in most of what Mr Brown said. Alex had faith in Vishwaroopaha, and Vishwaroopaha seemed to have faith in Mr Brown.

To drift himself away from this topic, Alex tilted behind Mr Brown and peeped over his shoulder, hoping to catch a glimpse at the thing Mr Brown was looking for in his pocket. Did he prepare a speech, and had forgotten the lines?

Sure enough, he took out a rectangular piece of paper, though it was scrunched up, and very small. There was no way the words he had *already* spoken could've even fitted on such a small piece of paper. The words written on it were in a very scrawly handwriting. Just the name VISHWAROOPAHA had been scribbled in capital letters.

Alex wondered why had that been written… Had Mr Brown forgotten Vishwaroopaha's name? Or... Was his name *not* Vishwaroopaha? Alex was so lost in his thoughts that he didn't realize he had been tilting on the extreme left, and almost fell from his surfboard. Mr Brown helped him correct his posture, and continued, 'Ah, so... What was I saying? Yeah, you must not visit the deadly realm, even if Vishwaroopaha asks you to do so. I know he's my master nowadays, but I ought to tell you what is "right". After all, that's what *Veeshwaerupeha* told me to do. "Tell them what is right," he had said'.

Mr Brown hadn't pronounced Vishwaroopaha's name correctly the second time, which made Alex doubt that Droller had frequently been using this term. But another thought suddenly took over Alex's mind, 'Yeah, obviously, he wouldn't—He's Vishwaroopaha's servant. He has probably always addressed Vishwaroopaha as "Sir" or "Master"'.

'So, anyway, that's primary information, I'll tell you all more once we get to Sternind. We'll have a cup of Liquechloro there, okay? That'll be relaxing. Now, be ready to go through your last few hours on Earth today, because boy, I tell you, they ain't gonna be easy. We're heading for the land near the Antarctic Circle, since the portal to Sternind is there. But first... We'll need to have a pit stop in that snowy landmass, just to fuel up these Aviaboards. Oh and try not to think too much… We don't need a large gas canister for refuelling these, just a bit of RP. You will be okay with that, won't you? We'll be there for almost an hour, and I'll help you be more or less *okay* in that weather, so don't worry. You may try the best to not freeze yourself to death, `cause we're in for a cold day!'

Chapter 2

A Reckless Bargain

The first question – among a million others – in Alex's mind was, 'What is RP?' Though it seemed just like a short form of "Regular Price" or "Red Phosphorous" or "Role Play" or whatever, Alex sensed some importance in just those two letters. He wondered what would happen if he got to know its full form. He just hoped that saying that word's full form wasn't prohibited, for if it too dispelled high frequency terror waves.

After moving about in the sky for a few more hours, Alex felt the sun shining brightly, forcing him to provide shade to his eyes with his hand. A few moments later, massive snowy landmass came into view when he tried to look downwards.

A rough landing wasn't what Alex had expected. He had assumed that those surfs would land vertically on the snow, allowing Alex to safely hand them over to

Mr Brown. But it turned out to be different. As soon as they got near a few meters of the snowy ground, the surfboards dissolved under their feet to turn into green coloured vapour, which gathered a few metres away and hardened into a bunch of keys. It fell onto the ground with a loud *clink*.

While Mr Brown landed softly on both his feet, Alex fell down *really* hard. His muscles groaned. His bones felt weak, as if cracking. Alex stood up, sneezed about a million times and looked around. The cold was intense. He wrapped his arms around himself. Lester and Angelina were just starting to get on their feet. Mr Brown was fiddling with his bunch of keys, making some weird hand movements around it as if he was enchanting it with magic, which Alex thought to be RP. He just hoped that Mr Brown would get off his funny business and help him and his friends, at least a little.

Suddenly, Mr Brown's jaw dropped. Again, he had that look of a school boy on his face, but apparently for something other than the examination. Maybe the student had forgotten to bring his Tiffin.

He came over and helped Lester stand up on his feet. He said, with a look on his face as if he was going to blurt out **Damn it! I've forgotten something. Is it my pair of trousers?** any second, 'Look, you three, we've run into a slight problem here. Actually, I've forgotten... Um...'

Alex thought of jeering in an accusing manner, completing Mr Brown's sentence ...**your trousers? I don't think they're here. Wanna have some cool sky-teleporting flames in your face?**

Perhaps with some nice "Control Yourself" devices? but then ruled the idea out of his mind. He really needed to concentrate on keeping himself warm and on Mr Brown's… *casual-but-shocking* way of speaking.

'...A very essential thing to refuel our Aviaboards for us to get going. So you all need to help me with that. See, it is a little plastic gun that fires snow. Sounds weird, eh? I know... By the way, I have no idea how to get it here, or somehow *make* it,' said Mr Brown, straightforwardly saying all this as if trying to signal **Hey, you three! I've got you all (including me) in a mess! I bet we can't wriggle out of it! So now, let's happily die here!**

Angelina almost jumped out of shock, which was clearly visible as it spread across her face. Alex remembered the "coldy-guy" gun she had obtained from somewhere at Wasor Island. She hadn't coughed up the story of how she had got all those guns even when she was asked about it by any of her parents or friends. Maybe it was the same way Alex had won those badges after completion of the tasks. *That* "coldy-guy" gun's description and features were the similar as Mr Brown had said, and Alex wondered if it was the same thing.

Angelina overtook Alex in coming up with an idea for something—again. 'I think I know how to get this… gun. But it'll have to be just one of us. There are chances of… Something going very… *very* wrong.'

'Now you're talking!' said Mr Brown, with a smile spreading on his face.

'Um...' Alex interrupted, shivering in the cold. 'I bet

you didn't c-care to listen to what sh-she said last, Mr Brown.'

'Bah! That's nonsense! I can handle dangerous stuff with RP. I think you must learn it too. Well, of course, you *will*, and we're gonna talk about that later. But for now, let's focus on the task at hand. We'll get through this. Rather, *I'll* get through this. Angelina, dear, tell me what I have to do.'

'Excuse me,' Angelina said as she walked away with Mr Brown.

'Whaddya thin-in-k-k th-that is?' Lester asked, stammering due to the cold. He scooted up over to Alex.

'Um... I guess, whatever it is, it's not g-good. Yeah, y-you're shivering too? I-It's only going to get w-worse. So l-let's ask Mr Brown to g-get us a little bit of f-fire.'

Lester just smiled and moved away weakly to ask Mr Droller Brown for some aid.

A few minutes later, Alex found himself near a fire, kindled on large tree trunks – which materialized out of nowhere – by Mr Brown with those weird hand movements, with Angelina and Lester also around the flames trying to warm themselves. Mr Brown had strolled off somewhere to get the "coldy-guy".

Alex looked around him. Lester was busy warming his hands. Angelina was sitting next to the fire on the snow with her hands wrapped around her legs; her head resting on her knees. When she eventually looked up, though, she seemed pretty glum. For a long time, no one uttered a single word. Alex knew for sure that everyone was trying to digest all that Mr Droller had said.

Alex thought of starting a conversation; since the "coldy-guy" topic had come up, Alex decided to ask Angelina about her experience with the guns, to try and lessen the grief that had apparently accompanied her memory.

'Sharing about your unpleasant experiences with friends lessens up the emotional burden, Angelina. Tell me how you got those plastic guns. Without your suffering in getting the "coldy-guy" and that gun we'd used to reduce the size of the Prime Lever, we could've done nothing.'

'Hmm...' she took a shaky breath. 'It'll be hard to believe...'

'For me, not at all. I think what *I* went through is harder to believe. But I told you all about it, didn't I? You okay with that reasoning?'

Angelina shrugged and rested her head again on her knees. Though her face was partly visible, Alex could notice a little smirk tug at corner of her mouth. 'Anyway,' he said. 'Now come on. Tell us.'

He then looked at Lester for support. 'Oh, yeah. You may...' he said and went back to warming his hands again.

Angelina sat up straight. Alex hadn't noticed earlier, but by the looks of her face, it seemed as if she had been silently crying till a few minutes before. He decided not to bring up the topic.

'It so happened,' Angelina started. 'When the fifth challenge almost ended, I was hit by a large rock, and separated from both of you. I don't know how I was saved, but I found myself in a forest, my T-Shirt soaked in blood. It was… painful...'

Alex gave her some time to gather herself. Even he had had such a depressing attitude, whenever he had to narrate the story of the first level of the seventh challenge at Wasor. He had been encircled and gripped tightly by strong, green root-like structures which squeezed him until all the blood was drained out of his body. If it hadn't been for that *three-lives* concept, he would've surely died.

In this situation, though, he figured that the only way to help Angelina in not *breaking from within* was to apply the *Lester-method*—Jokes. He said with reference to what Angelina had said a few moments before, 'Blood... Yeah, you know what, I too have had personal experience with that thing. All of it was squeezed out of me that time...' Alex didn't know how to transform this into a joke. So he settled with silly stuff. 'You know, it tickled! And I felt good, too...'

What happened was unexpected. Angelina first stared for a good five seconds, probably not knowing what to make of such a statement. She then flashed a big goofy smile, and said in an overly sarcastic tone, 'You're silly. Anyone ever tell you that?'

Not jokes, but stupidity did the trick.

Angelina continued narrating, 'I moved around in the forest, edging away from suspicious sounds, rustles in the leaves... Some stuff you typically find in movies, not ordinary forests. But that was Wasor Island, after all. No hope was left at all for me, no energy... My knees buckled and I fell onto the ground, and my head hit something cold, in such a hot and humid forest... Then–'

Alex sparked up with a joke—Sort of. 'You know what... I had also noticed something that was warm in a cold weather. Though it is different, it *is* a weird change. You see, it was this gooey brown-black thing like pig sludge, and when I fed it to Lester...'

Lester reacted quickly, a mixed look of frustration and anger spreading over his face. 'What!? How did...?' Alex hadn't told him or anyone else about that thing he'd used to cure Lester after he suffered a serious concussion. He'd just assured everyone that it was a miracle that Lester had woken up by himself after their great fall from that *volcano explosion*.

Angelina didn't look amused, rather more solemn. Alex asked her sympathetically, 'What was it, Angelina? You don't seem okay at all... I mean, not that we both are okay with what's happening, but you seem a bit more... Kind of... Depressed.'

'It's– It's nothing. I... I just don't like cold. I swear, I'll be the first one ready to get out of here when – *if* – Mr Brown returns... Alive.'

'Just tell us whatever's bothering you, Angelina, don't be shy,' Alex said, trying to ignore the last sentence said by her.

'Yeah, okay, you want to know the truth, then I'll shove it in your face! I just didn't want you both to be like me... "Depressed", you say. But now, YOU

DESERVE IT! Bugging me a lot... There you go! When I fell on the ground, my vision spun, and I found myself, though alright– not bloody, but in a worse condition, in a place, where the surroundings were… Well, icy. I mean, everything was ice– I was in an endless corridor, with no doors of rooms, no lights, nothing. My vision was blue. The ground beneath me was frosty ice. The walls of the corridor were icy blue. Cold waves – Like the ones attacking your face when you open the freezer door – circled me, swirling in and out of my mouth and nostrils... I ran through the hallway, tiring myself with only an endless icy way to walk on... I bid goodbye to life and everyone—Including you both dodos, and decided to depart from life, in for some heaven sort-of thing.'

Alex commented, 'I too, have once gone bananas. But that was when I wasn't able to find a way out of a *burning* tent. Is it a coincidence, or some plan, that you and me were assigned the same kind of tasks, but with opposite themes?'

'Exactly... That's what I was trying to figure out, when you said I was *depressed*. It's all fishy... Who could possibly be behind all this...'

Alex had a weird thought. He said, 'Vishwaroopaha...?'

'Oh, come on. Uncle Edward, or Mr V is just a foodie. How could he... Anyway, I wouldn't mind it if I tell you the rest of my experiences in brief... Will *you* mind?'

'Of course not,' Alex replied with little chuckle, happy that Angelina was readily opening up about the incident.

'Looking around, I found a source of light. You know what they say... A sparkling light of knowledge always helps you in darkness of ignorance. In my case, it was white light reaching me even in the icy blueness. It led me to a room, where, through some kind of a *virtual-reality-hallucination* tech, questions judging my wisdom were asked to me. Most painful of all, I was shown situations. In one of them, I was humiliated by both of you really badly; you were abusing me... You and Lester... and then, I saw a something... Something I had never ever thought in even in my dreams would have ever happened... You were good friends with Peter Colter, that football bully. He was there with you and Lester, instead of me. Then I was asked a question that whether I really liked you two as my friends...'

'So you said no, then. This is quite a lot to shake a person badly. I am surprised how you are in one piece.'

'It's nice of you to try and make me feel better, Alex—I've been noticing that. You said the obvious thing which I did. All I said is "No" angrily. But later, I told myself it was otherwise. One gets a lot of time to regret. That place was devilish. I begged that guy to let me go; he said he would, and bargained with me.'

'Which guy? Who was actually torturing you like that?'

'There was this demon behind all of it. I'll tell you more about him in a while. For now, listen as I narrate. I seriously don't like interruptions.'

'Oh, alright.'

'So he bargained–'

'For what? A bony guy was bargaining with me too. He was offering me an entry to the ninth challenge, in lieu of my soul. I crushed that man under rubble.'

'I said no interruptions,' Angelina said, looking annoyed.

'Sorry.'

'I can't believe how I let go, but I accepted his offer. I was desperate, and there was no other way. That demon presented me with those guns and said that they were very helpful. He let me go to your ninth challenge, but with a curse—He would live inside me, as a parasite. The reason for that, as he said, was that he was "fragment of a lone soul". He said that whenever you guys need me the most, he would bring out the worst in me. That's what I had turned into after rescuing Lester. This demon...' Angelina said something like *K-LOAD-BOR-EE-OD* and signed ***CLOEDBORIOGD*** in ASL, which Alex understood fluently. She continued, 'That's what I think his name spells like. If… If he comes up again, promise me, that you'll not hesitate in… *neutralizing* me. Otherwise... That would be our weakness.'

'Lester and I are incomplete without you, Angelina. So, I'm not going to promise you that. We'll surely find a way without you at that time. We'll be prepared. Besides, that's not even true right now, what you said about Cloedboriogd. All the things related to the challenges had been destroyed, disappeared into nothing after our dads pulled it down together.'

'No, Alex. That isn't it. The one who had made the challenges had decided death for anyone in my situation. I was failing in my tests. I would have been dead right there in the forest, if I had been trying to get through my trials, and not taken a detour for safety. I was on the verge of dying. But… Cloedboriogd saved me from that situation. He just came out of the blue. He was not related to the challenges at all, I tell you. He was somehow there when we were at Wasor, and is still here. So, anyway, he then he tested me with his questions. I don't know what the result of the answers was, but Cloedboriogd finally accepted me. I don't know why he decided to live inside me, but my instincts told me that it was just right. I had felt a burden upon my shoulders when he had gotten inside me, and that feeling was active until today. Cloedboriogd wasn't fooling around. Even though he hasn't acted yet, he *is* real, much more deadly than anything we've *ever* seen, I guess. And if Mr Brown's words about that deadliest realm are true, then I guess Cloedboriogd comes from there.'

'Right now I only have one suggestion for you, Angelina. Do *not* give in to whatever that beast asks you to do. Oh and speaking of Mr Brown, what exactly did you ask him to do?'

'I just told him to mutter curses for Cloedboriogd, and he would have his gun. That demon really likes making deals, and I was certain he would be drawn to Mr Brown if he heard something against himself. It seemed like Mr Brown already knew about Cloedboriogd, but was still intrigued by how I knew a way of making the demon useful. As if the plan worked, I got rid of that sensation of Cloedboriogd inside me. Mr Brown is dealing with him now, and... **Aah! Cloed... He has got hold of me again... Wonder what Mr Brown has sacrificed to get the gun...'**

Alex felt really bad for Angelina. He knew how such a burden felt. He had been *very* keen to get rid of it. And when he finally had, it felt like heaven—All wishes fulfilled. He thought, 'Poor Angelina. She's just... Broken. Now, when she's got the demon on herself again, I just hope Mr Brown shows up soon with his weird "facts", or Angelina will...'

As if God had listened to his *Angelina-must-not-explode* prayer pretty well, Mr Brown came walking towards them, a frown spread across his face. He was encircled by warm light; maybe that was his magic. His right eye was covered by an eye patch. 'So *that's* what Mr Brown has sacrificed... His eye. They are more precious than anything... But why does Cloedboriogd ask for weird things? He has eyes, he has his own demon body... What is it he's planning to do with things he had got from Mr Brown and Angelina...'

'RP didn't do the trick, Angelina. You were right,' Mr Brown said; his temper had changed a lot. It had totally transformed from casual to grumpy.

'So now, let's not pay much attention to this... sudden change in my appearance. Don't even ask me about it. Let's move after I refuel our Aviaboards,' Mr Brown said as he started making those hand movements again, sometimes taking out "coldy-guy" out of a duffel bag he'd brought with him when he'd showed up, and spewing a bit of ice-frosting on it. Alex wondered why did he specifically ask for that frost-dispensing gun even when he had a lot of snow available. After all, they were in Antarctica.

'So,' Mr Brown said after he'd done all his "hocus-pocus" around the keys and successfully changed them into surfboards... Or *Aviaboards* again. 'Now, let's move. Ah, a last warning I'd forgotten... Most people remain stunned for a day or two after they travel from one realm to the other. I hope you all better not, because if you are found blacked out for more than two days, it's a pure sign of what we Sternindians call getting shocked-up. I hope y'all aren't *that* weak, are you?' After a slight grin, he continued within a second, 'There will be a sudden change in surroundings. So, I request you to not be tense and stressed when you try to enter Sternind. Just think that it's all a Roller Coaster ride and shout "Whoa!" when the time comes... You'll feel as if you have been yanked out of your body and put back in again. Just be prepared.'

'I am prepared, Mr Brown,' Alex said, smiling as everyone climbed onto each of their Aviaboards. 'In fact, I actually have once been yanked out of my body and put back in again...'

Chapter 3

Liquechloro Liquefies

Alex was not prepared at all. As everyone's Aviaboards started flying vertically upward, Alex too turned at a right angle from the ground.

He didn't fall off; rather stayed put to the Aviaboard as his feet were buckled to it by *suddenly-appearing-out-of-nowhere-maybe-out-of-the-Aviaboard* curved metal plates. They were moving so fast in a ninety-degree position that Alex couldn't even feel the pain of the pressure exerted by the metal plates due to gravity. Alex looked around and noticed his friends along with Mr Brown. The same was everybody's condition– Vertical.

As everyone darted upwards at a great speed, Alex saw a pale blue layer of the sky. By this time, Alex had found it difficult to breathe. He started concentrating on the surroundings—to avoid losing consciousness. He noticed the Aviaboards heading for a spot where the pale blue layer was less dense. He had had enough of the cold air rushing past him.

Soon, he could take no more. He looked around. The warm light was still glowing around Mr Brown, and he seemed fine as he muttered something under his breath. Alex assumed it to be some kind of code word or spell, necessary to get into Sternind. His eyes drifted towards his friends. They were unconscious, latched to their Aviaboards by those curved metal plates. Their backs were bent backwards at seemingly impossible angles, all credit to Earth's gravitational force.

Alex too lost hope and decided to black out, confused whether this was a trap planned by Mr Brown and Vishwaroopaha to kill him and his friends by throwing them off those Aviaboards, or if Sternind was a real thing and what Mr Brown has said was actually going to happen. There were high chances of dying in both the situations.

Part of Alex wanted to somehow help his friends and get safely back home, *after* he had strangled Mr Brown. Though that wasn't possible, the mere thought made Alex feel a lot more relaxed than the "Roller Coaster" idea Mr Brown had suggested. He closed his eyes, ready to face what was going to happen.

Alex woke up in a house, sunlight peeping through the windows. He was curled up on the floor, biting the red rug. He quickly spat the taste out of his mouth as he stood up, feeling quite dizzy. It seemed like he was in the guest room of the house. The walls were the colour of polished wood. There was a television on the wall facing a glass table in the center of the room, around which were sofas also made up of... Transparent glass. There were framed photos of Mr Droller Brown with marvellous landscapes on the walls, except that the frames were also... made up of glass. The lamps on the walls weren't turned on; the room was just lit by sunlight. There was also a glass staircase leading to the first floor. He looked around, and found that he was alone. There was an unlatched door – also made up of glass – located at one end of the room. He quickly headed for it and yanked it open. The glass door didn't feel like glass. Instead, it felt like a normal wooden door.

He found himself in an open area, free from buildings. It was a large green well-maintained lawn with a walking track circling it. Mr Brown, Lester and Angelina were having a casual walk on the track, talking. Alex ran towards them, delighted to see them again.

As he reached them, stumbling – due to the light -headed feeling – he turned towards Lester to say something, but Mr Brown addressed him first. 'Come, my wonderful boy. You are officially accepted by the Realm's nature – *Sternind*'s nature – from where you'll be learning RP. Now, as you've been decided capable of handling RP—Realm Power responsibly, I must get your attention to some important points, which you really need to know before stepping foot into the streets of Sternind. First of all, it's not permitted for an adult who does not have thorough knowledge of RP to roam freely in the streets of Sternind. So, that's what you all need to decide... Are you smart enough to let yourself be turned into teenagers and receive your education here, or... Are you ready to get back to Earth with another hardship, just like the one you have faced to get into Sternind? But again, you might think it's all up to you three. The real question is—*Is it*, though? Now, go inside my house and decide, while I pick out some natural ingredients for the Liquechloro I promised you three.'

'Hmm...' Lester said. 'Mr Brown, could you please tell us that why the hell did you and Vishwaroopaha plan to get us here... All the while explaining to us all about this Sternind and stuff?'

'Er...' Mr Brown replied. 'First of all, I don't have any idea about my master's plans. Secondly, I bet you all heard what Vashweerupehaa had said—All by fate, to fate and for fate. Now go, and I don't want any more questions.'He looked stubborn so Alex decided not to get under his skin. Lester scowled at Mr Brown as he followed Alex and Angelina back to the living room.

As Alex settled himself on the glass sofa facing Lester, he was surprised to find it soft and comfy rather than hard and cold—It *was* unusual. But then, Sternind and the 'Realm' concept was weird too, much like the cold flames.

Lester seemed to be in a trance as he stared deep into some void of his own imagination, but was woken up by a sudden pat on the back by Angelina, who was sitting next to him.

'Hmm,' Lester said. 'I hate it. Bad idea... Very bad idea... Changed into teens again just because we need to do something in this *Sternind* and be here for a very long time… Also, what will happen in Florida? How do we know this is a place called *Sternind*? What's the proof that there's no dungeon right outside this house? How do we know we haven't been kidnapped?'

'I think we'll have to just trust two people – one who we barely know and the other who met us just a while back – on such an important matter. We don't have any other choice. But just… Come to think of it, there's a plus point in all this,' Angelina said. 'You know what, we *can* think about it. We'll control ourselves in Florida by those clones. We don't grow when we're adults, right? So, until we grow till adulthood here, in Sternind, we can stay, and control our adult selves back in Florida. We'll get to Earth again as adults after learning about all this "Realm Power" concept. Our parents won't have a hint of it.'

Alex checked his wristwatch. It wasn't there. He obviously hadn't put it on before getting to bed. 'Any idea what time is it? I think we need to control our clones back in Florida. It has been more than a day with us being unconscious, right? If so... We haven't woken up for a day in Florida. I just hope Vishwaroopaha has handled everything until now. He must've known about what we were going to face.'

'You're right,' Angelina said. 'Which makes me even

more tensed. I think we need to pay some time to those CY devices.'

'But then here's the problem,' Lester said. 'That being changed into teenagers thing... I just can't understand how to make use of time... Dwell on this topic or set off to use the CY devices?'

Alex thought about it. 'I think I have an idea. Both issues might be solved. First, we'll accept becoming teenagers again. In doing so, we'll extend our life experiences by a few years. Wonder how this Realm Power changes the laws of nature, by turning us into teens...'

Lester questioned, 'What's second, though?'

'Secondly,' Alex replied. 'We'll accept that Liquechloro Mr Brown is offering us and tell him our decision. Then we'll have a bit of rest playing our part in Florida.'

Angelina turned towards Alex and gave him a look like *I don't feel very good about this*. She looked like she was about to throw up on the rug. In reply, Alex made a gesture indicating *We'll talk later. Just wait.*

'Well, then,' Lester said, getting up, apparently aware about Alex and Angelina's silent conversation. 'I'll just bring Mr Brown here. I don't like the very sound of the word *Liquechloro*. It sounds like a well-known brand of poison.' As Lester went out of the room through the glass door.

Angelina exhaled heavily after Lester had left. 'Hmm... I just... I hate it this way. It's too much…'

Alex felt awful for Angelina again. She had just begun her college days and was driven into all this… Wasor,

Sternind and now Cloedboriogd.

Angelina said firmly, 'I can't understand how to let go. We have just been whisked away from our homes. And really, Lester has started making a lot of sense... We've been kidnapped. Now the kidnapper is saying that he'll turn us into teens, and the reason is simply just *fate*. We should have had a one-hour discussion on this topic, but we whipped through it in just five minutes...? That's completely... Insane.'

'What can we do about it? Nothing. We can't even try to sneak back to Earth, even if we found how to. I do *not* want to get through that pale blue stuff in the air.'

'Ozone.'

'Wait, *what*?'

'The ozone hole. That's what we've come through. Mr Brown told us.'

'That's... I mean, we couldn't survive there... There's simply no chance that this "Realm Power" can overwrite science concepts...'

'*That's* what I call insane. It's just... We have to face everything unwillingly. I'm tired of things like this. Wasor shook me up badly, and now it's all this *Realm* stuff,' Angelina said. A few seconds later, she said with a deep thinking expression, 'How about we don't?'

'What do you mean?'

'What if we don't go with all this baloney, huh? We do have a choice to go back, right? It might just take a few days of unconsciousness, that's it. But at least it'll be better than forcibly having our whole *courses of life* altered.'

'You don't think I already thought of that?' replied Alex. 'Mr Brown did say "*Is it*, though?" when he gave us the choice. Which totally changes my interpretation of this "choice" given to us. I mean, just look at all this stuff. If Mr Brown and Vishwaroopaha had to give us a choice in the end, they wouldn't have taken so much pains to even get us here in the first place. This "choice" thing is just a formality, I guess. To make them look humble and make us believe that we have ourselves chosen to be in Sternind as teenagers, and not forced.'

Angelina took Alex by surprise when she said, 'Alex, that's not a believable cause, okay? You can't just go around and *find* reasons to stay here. I know there's something you're not telling me. Your expression says it all. Now it's time for *you* to cough up some stuff, bozo.'

'No, it's nothing,' Alex said, trying to give a fake reassuring smile. He didn't want to tell Angelina about what Vishwaroopaha had done in Florida to force Alex to go with Mr Brown. And just like an obedient little fool, Alex had for some reason convinced his friends, too. He truly felt regret.

Alex was thinking of a way to take all this lightly. He was ready to believe that Lester would – at that very moment – get in the room with a broad smile on his face. **It's all fake!**, he would say. **There's no such thing as a Realm! This was a magical prank! We're all good!** But no such thing happened. Even the sunlight entering the room gave a sad vibe, as if saying, **Sadly, my friend, this is all genuine.**

'We must have courage, and for now, believe this to be

the truth. For some time, we'll learn this "Realm Power", and we'll be good to go! It'll be a whole new experience, Angelina. Why worry about something else if you have something better...' Alex said after a long silence.

'It's *not* better,' Angelina replied, her nostrils flaring. 'Florida was a lot better—*home* was a lot better. We don't even know this place. And we're being turned into teens to spend some *years* of our life here. No one seems to care about if and how we suffer and what we think.'

'You're right, but we need to cope up. We need to blend in the surroundings, and not be the ones who stand out in, er– a negative way. We have to try to be like the *common* people here.'

'Hm.'

Internally, Alex was deeply disturbed. There was simply no chance that "Realm Power" was something more logical or genuine than science. 'Even if it is, then why did Mr Brown refer to it as RP on Earth? And as soon as he gets in Sternind, it's all "Realm Power",' Alex muttered, not realizing that he had said it out aloud.

Mr Brown, who apparently heard him, said, as he moved towards Alex with three bone china cups with floral prints on a tray in his hands, 'That, is secondary information boy, which I said that I would tell you later. Now is the time for something else. You wanted to know about RP, right? So listen, the name has a lot of power. Common names like Alex, Lester and Angelina don't show any characteristics of power, as they're so commonly used that their uniqueness and qualities have been stripped off. But "Realm Power", when said out aloud on Earth, summons a lightning strike, powerful enough to kill the speaker. Because that's the punishment for leaking the secrets of Sternind and the third Realm to the inhabitants of Earth. Any one of the three Realms can make use of Realm Power, but not the ones who're totally believing in and dependent on this so-called *science*.' Lester was behind him, looking tensed.

'Can I go through this "lightning" experience if I just happen to say the word accidentally? You know what I mean... It isn't something a normal resident of Earth won't be ever able to come up with. When I am on Earth, if I mistakenly spill out the two words instead of the short form from my mouth, then is there any kind of defence technique? Some special spell?' Lester asked as he and Mr Brown seated themselves.

'Do you consider Realm Power some teeny-weeny magic stuff? It's a lot more complicated. Not just some silly concept stating that we need a wand and some spells to perform the so-called *magic*.' Mr Brown replied, uttering the last word with absolute disgust.

'So, what you Sternindians perform isn't magic? I mean, you say it's Realm Power, which I guess straightforwardly states that any person of the Realm can get to know this power and use it. But from where exactly do you get this power?'

Mr Brown smiled. 'I think I'll leave that to the Sternind Institute of Realm Power learning. For short, SIRP. You'll all learn your hidden skills there.'

Before anyone else could say something, Alex came up with a reasonable question for Mr Brown. He said, 'You said, if we name a dimension, it creates another one. You people had made the mistake of naming Sternind, so the third deadliest Realm was created. But now you say that the third Realm also has a name, and you embroider the foolish fact with lots of "terror waves" stuff. My question is, if the third Realm also has a name, then why don't we have a fourth realm?'

'That's the technicality, boy. I'm a graduate of Titleology, from SIRP. I know many things about this "name" concept. Broadly, I can say that if the name's not used commonly, in our case, the fourth Realm can't be formed.'

'I see. That's why you people came up with the stupid term "high frequency terror waves" to prevent people from saying that word.'

'Unfortunately, you're right.'

There was silence for a long time after that. For Alex, this all was hard to believe until he saw the truth himself. He guessed that it was the same thought his friends were longing to rely on—to deny that this "Realm" Concept was real.

'Here, have some Liquechloro,' Mr Brown said, passing each of them a cup. 'It tastes awesome. Maybe it'll even help you all get rid of that giddy sensation after inter-Realm travel.'

Alex felt so hungry he emptied the whole cup in a single gulp. It was a green liquid, that tasted pretty good.

It was sweet, with a hint of spicy flavour. By looking at it, someone could've mistaken it for a sour spinach'n'herbs smoothie.

'And, I do warn you, don't drink it all rapidly. You have to take your time to drink it. Enjoy the taste slowly. Otherwise, there'll be a tissue and bone contraction in your bod...' Mr Brown said, faltering, as he caught a glimpse of the spot behind Alex. 'Oh god.'

Suddenly, the room expanded. Lester and Angelina's bellies started bulging—turning them into massive balloons. Alex suspected that someone behind him must be radiating their power, making his friends larger and larger – almost about to explode – leaving him and Mr Brown in the living room for some kill-off. Alex stayed completely still.

Alex needed not more than a second to realize that the room wasn't getting bigger, but he was getting smaller. Mr Brown's words confirmed it. His eyes didn't have tissues in them, so they stayed the same, and that's why his sight was so messed up. Everything he looked at was perfectly oval. A minute later, he found it hard to focus on his eyesight. He tried to look around, but couldn't move his neck. He couldn't feel it, as if it wasn't there. Each part of his body except his face was numb, as if it had ceased to exist. A couple minutes later, the numbness reached his mouth, and he decided to take a quick glimpse of his surroundings before turning into something… Un-human.

Alex noticed his height had shrunk to the level of

the glass table top. Because of the numbness, he hadn't noticed that he had slid down the sofa and turned into something liquid. He wondered what his friends and Mr Brown would do for him, if anything. He hadn't heard the screams or yelps of his friends, and instinctively guessed that they might've also liquefied. He hoped that Mr Brown would pitch in. Before giving them Liquechloro, he might've planned some safety measures, some aid. Alex gathered the courage and strength to look as high up as possible from his low elevation "liquefied" position. Sure enough, there were two more greenish-black slime like liquid figures plopped on the red rug. Angelina and Lester had fully crumbled into green slop. Also, Mr Brown was… smiling?

Just then, he had the time to think of one other thing before his brain liquefied—Was it something other than the realms that Mr Brown and Vishwaroopaha had planned for them...?

It clicked him, which was the obvious thing in such a situation.

Treachery was what Alex hated the most.

Chapter 4

Alexander the ~~Great~~

Being liquefied wasn't painful. Alex just felt physically and emotionally numb. A second went by. Then another. He came back to consciousness, his vision spinning.

He woke up as his normal self, thankful that his size hadn't permanently changed to that of an ant's. He was expecting himself to be locked up in a prison cell. Instead, he was right where he'd liquefied. He stood warily, and noticed something strange—he had transformed into a teen. His clothes had also been changed to an elegant black formal suit.

Ah, shit... Surely Mr Brown had taken advantage of "Tissue and Bone contraction" to turn Alex and his friends into teens.

Alex had always been aware of his age. When he was young, he longed to grow up. But when he finally grew up, he figured that being a kid was way better than being an adult. There were lesser responsibilities, and a lot more *child-like* happy moments. The very thought made him smile. He decided that, what had happened wasn't so bad after all. He had just been… changed. BUT WHY, THOUGH? Why without prior warning? With amazement came curiosity.

Not forgetting his friends, he rushed through the glass door into the open lawn and took a quick look around. The sky was slowly turning bluish-black from yellowish-orange.

He spotted his teen friends sitting in the lawn, talking. Mr Brown wasn't there. Alex didn't even try to guess where he was. All he cared about then was his friends. They too were dressed like him, in black suits. He rushed towards them and plopped himself on the ground next to Lester. 'So, what are our ages now?'

Angelina replied, first gesturing towards Alex, then Lester, and finally herself, 'Well, according to Mr Brown… Fifteen, fourteen and *twelve*.'

Alex couldn't believe what Angelina had said. They had earlier been twenty-one, twenty and eighteen. So they would have to spend *six* years in this "Realm" stuff? He said, anger filling his throat which later turned to despair, 'How dare he do that!? He has stretched this thing to six years! I would've tolerated it to three years back, but it's six! I–'

Lester cut him off. 'Can we help it?'

'No, but–'

'*Can* we change it?'

'I don't–'

'Don't be like that. We've already been through all this. Just be… you know, *optimistic*.'

'Right,' Alex said grudgingly.

Angelina said, 'Well, I'll take off from here now. I'll just... you know, try to digest all this. If anyone needs company, I'm ready to help. Come over, I'll be watching Sternind's cable TV.'

She got up and started walking towards the glass door, muttering, 'Come on, *twelve – year – old – and – not – even – a – teen – Angelina*. Let's watch television, even when you've been treated like a lab rat for some "Changing adults into smaller than teens spell"…'

Alex felt really bad for Angelina for the third time that day. She had suffered so much and needed some time away from all this. And that's what she'd apparently went off to enjoy—A *break*.

Alex excused himself, saying, 'I'll check out those CY devices...' though that wasn't why he wanted to get away from Lester. He just decided to leave Lester and Angelina alone, giving them time to digest the recent events.

He went up the second floor through the glass stairs, ignoring Angelina who was fiddling with the TV remote control, probably trying to figure out how to turn it on.

He had just leaned against a wall near the topmost step of the staircase, not caring about his surroundings – just *despairing* – when Mr Brown showed up out of nowhere, and shouted in his face, 'Ta-da!'

Alex was frightened by the sudden appearance of Mr Brown so much that he almost tumbled down the stairs.

'You're kidding, right?' Alex asked Mr Brown apprehensively.

But Mr Brown himself seemed puzzled by Alex's question. 'Kidding `bout what?'

'Not here. Not in your house. Not at all in my friends' presence. Somewhere else. Let's talk somewhere outside.'

'Hmm, what's the time?' Mr Brown asked, but then realized that Alex wasn't wearing a wristwatch. He checked his own. 'Ho-hum. It's 9:00 o'clock now, so... I think *The Walking Talks* might be open. Let's head there. I can't wait to have a chocolate statue...'

Unnoticed by Lester or Angelina, as they stepped out of the main gate, Alex saw a wide street alive with traffic in front of him. There were old-fashioned and intricately carved designs on the streetlamps which burned yellow on both sides of the lane. The road and the buildings were modernized, but were made up of black, shiny rock. At night, the place looked amazing.

Except… Some things were weird. People were dressed like Mr Brown, in common outfits, but they were not moving anywhere in cars, or motorcycles, or even magical flying broomsticks. They were each sitting on some or the other self-moving invisible thing, patting it with hands somewhere or the other, talking to it somehow, while it worked as a vehicle for them. For some people, the invisible thing was of short height, so it hoisted the rider a bit less up in the air. Whereas, some people were soaring high up.

If technically guessed, those things must've been larger and broader than the people riding them, and thus, they might've been covering more space on the street. There were so many people in the airspace of the lane that if the invisible things were even of the least possible assumed size, judging by the denseness of the people present, they should've bumped into each other, leading to major accidents. But that didn't happen. Alex's mouth hung open as he marvelled at the science, the "Realm Power" and the weirdness of this place. He decided not to ask Mr Brown about all this since he'd probably give another long lecture or tell him to leave some things for SIRP.

Alex stopped focusing on the feeling of absolute amazement after seeing this *invisible thing* concept, and noticed the footpath busy with pedestrians on both sides of the road. It was made up of red-painted stone with a nice grip—perfect for walking. Unlike Mr Brown's house's slippery black outer walls.

'How far is the place we're heading to? Because what I'm talking about isn't any Pinkerton-level topic. I just need to discuss a thing or two,' Alex asked Mr Brown, breaking the long silence between them.

'Hmm... Pinkerton, you say? Never heard of it...'

'Probably because you're from Sternind,' Alex muttered.

'I beg your pardon?'

'Um... Could you please tell me how long it's going to take to get there?'

'Oh, we *are* there. Look to your left.'

Alex fixed his eyesight on the shop's title board.

The WALKING TALKS

Best quality food and drinks for all ages!

It was a two-storied restaurant made up of wood. It looked like a tree house, except it was on the ground. The entrance was a wooden door, on which hung a sign that read OPEN. The restaurant seemed too corny to Alex. He guessed that there may be too many people at this place and he wouldn't get a quiet spot to talk to Mr Brown. But he was hungry too. He decided to go in, but stopped himself.

He hadn't known that Mr Brown would lead him to a restaurant, without even asking Lester and Angelina about whether they were coming or not. But maybe Mr Brown had deliberately not said anything to them, as Alex wanted to talk to him alone. Plus, Lester and Angelina *did* look pretty glum and scowled at Mr Brown each time they saw him, probably trying to say **Don't come near me or I'll rip your face apart.**

Alex got in, wondering what "weird" things he would get to see again. He saw nothing but a three-walled room occupied by around ten glass capsule-like vehicles which moved over a rail track. Each one of them was large enough to carry three people. All this fit perfectly in the restaurant's brightly lit room. The track led the capsules outside the restaurant, where it split up into many tracks to allow two or more capsules to move at the same time.

'What *is* this?' Alex asked Mr Brown.

'Self-serve. Just get in the glass-rider first to move out, and set off to have a whole tour of Sternind. Food and drinks will be presented along the way. Pay at the end of the tour. If you didn't like something, get the refund.'

'Whoa... This seems quite good. A new type of leisure dining...' Alex replied, ready to go along with Mr Brown.

But then a thought occurred to him. 'But, you know, I'll need to bring Lester and Angelina here. Without them, I truly won't have as much fun. We are supposed to be together.'

'You think they would come with you? They're probably crying now. Don't know how to handle hard feelings...'

Anger bubbled inside Alex. Mr Brown had given Alex and his friends almost no protection in the cold region of Antarctica, let them be unconscious and didn't even bother to care for them; he turned them into teens without their permission; he decided that Alex's friends weren't worth a side excursion to a restaurant just because they showed some signs of hopelessness and now he was saying that his *friends* didn't know how to handle hard feelings? Alex knew for sure that Mr Brown had absolutely no idea about the hard feelings Lester and Angelina had handled.

Mr Brown had just brought them misery, and now he was blaming them for not being strong-hearted. If the same treatment was given to Mr Brown, he might have run away, wailing like a baby.

Alex wanted to smack Mr Brown on the head with a metal rod and shout, **See, this is a hard feeling. You must learn to get over it! Don't you want to? If you don't then I'll take you back to Earth! You're not even worth going to** The Walking Talks!

This was the feeling Alex's friends might've been experiencing, and he wanted Mr Brown to have a taste of his own medicine. But anyway, Alex climbed in one of the capsules. Mr Brown came in after him.

As soon as they got in, Mr Brown used Realm Power to activate the capsule. He made some hand movements around the inner surface of the glass, that made Alex wonder whether he was cleaning the glass with some invisible thing, instead of apparently *summoning* food.

Finally, after a few minutes or so, a robotic arm came out of nowhere and presented Alex with red sauce Penne pasta. It was a large plate, and the knife, forks and spoons were placed away from the dish in a tidy manner.

Alex started examining the intricate design of the fork.

'Wait. We must be patient enough to wait for the glass-rider to start moving, and pick up speed. It's the basics of eating at a place like this in Sternind,' Mr Brown interrupted.

'I didn't start ea–'

'It's the rules.'

'You mean table manners? Well, okay. And FYI, I didn't even start eating. So that unjust interruption of yours was… Well, unjust.'

Mr Brown didn't reply to that. He closed his eyes in deep concentration, and the glass capsule suddenly lurched forward. It headed outside the restaurant and followed the track into large grass fields and farms that seemed to go on forever. For all Alex knew, the surroundings weren't affecting the interior of this vehicle. In cars, as the automobile picks up speed, the passengers get pushed backward to their seats, because of inertia. But here, even when the glass capsule was moving with a fast speed, Alex and Mr Brown weren't pushed back to its glass walls. The Sternindians' act of overcoming and overwriting science concepts truly fazed Alex.

After fifteen minutes or so, the capsule (or glass-rider, as Mr Brown had said) came to a halt in front of a large lake. The sight was breathtaking. It was a view of the whole city. The landscape of this Sternindian city was more amazing than any other city he had seen. There were high rise buildings, mostly modern, but in some portions of the city, most of them were made up of shiny rock. They were not simple skyscrapers like some apartment or hotel, but many tall structures all joined together by various kinds of buildings. Alex noticed another astounding thing about them. Not just some of the buildings, but all of them were joined somehow. It was just like the Petronas Twin Towers, except the bridge connecting the towers was another modernized building hovering in the air, with some kind of an energy field below it which was noticeable as it looked like a swirling translucent green mist. Maybe this signified the character of the people here—They were joined, together, a team. Whatever this city was, by looking at it, Alex was dumbfounded.

He looked around him. From here, the track was spread out on both the sides where their capsule was, East and West. There were similar capsules parked on the tracks. *Other customers of The Walking Talks*, Alex guessed.

Forgetting the purpose of his talk or the question he was going to ask Mr Brown in the absence of his friends, he asked him something that was bugging him the most at the moment. 'Which city of Sternind is this?'

'Boy, in Sternind, there aren't cities. There're states, just states. Most Sternindians call them Prants.' He pronounced the word "Prant" like *pr-aah-n-t*.

Certainly not ready for learning new Sternindian terms like "Prants" which he didn't even know how to pronounce, Alex got to the point. He said, 'What made you rewind our ages back to *six* years?'

'Nothing but instincts. After all, learning how to make use of Realm Power takes six years for most people.'

'By saying *most*, do you mean there's no specific time duration for learning this Sternindian stuff? We can graduate from SIRP as soon as we've learned everything, right?'

'Technically, yes. But you can't do it alone before six years. If you want to get through it in less than six years, then... That depends on the coping up and learning rate of your supporters.'

'Supporters? You mean my friends, Lester and Angelina?'

'No, not them. In Sternind, you don't think of friends or family when hear the word "supporter". In Sternind, you are on your own, just having Supporters: One, your Article Of Power and two, your "Majenimal," that is like your buddy, your mate who helps you in all situations. If we talk about those people who were riding those invisible creatures... You know why they were invisible to you? Those creatures are called Majenimals. They are only visible to the ones who have passed a specific test in SIRP. Before that, they can only see their Majenimal, if they have one.'

'Hmm.'

'Majenimal stands for *majestic animal*, not *magical animal*, mind you. As for the set of Supporters, you'll have to receive your Supporters by getting through some tests that judge your character unless...'

Alex thought of those tests. He feared whether they will be just like another set of those ten challenges at Wasor. But the word *unless* gave him a spark of hope. His mind burning with curiosity, he spoke 'Unless what? Where are *your* Supporters?'

Mr Brown didn't answer Alex's second question, as if he hadn't heard it. Alex guessed maybe Mr Brown didn't have a good account of his past with his own Supporters.

But Mr Brown answered Alex's first question, 'Unless you inherit them. Which you can. This is not inheritance from any of your relatives or parents. You can inherit a Supporter from the person Sternind's RAA –

Realm Automatic Administration – has chosen for you. Realm Power attaches every new arrival in Sternind to a set of Supporters. You don't even know whether those Supporters are yet to be assigned to someone or they belong to someone who is already living in Sternind during the last days of his or her life.'

He continued, 'As soon as you enter Sternind, the person whose Supporter you are inheriting becomes emotionally detached to his or her Supporters and they get attached to you. The person feels an irresistible urge to give them, or it to you.'

'But what if the person who has the Supporters is dead?'

'One will never die with his Supporters. They will always be assigned to someone else before the owner's death.'

'Ohh.'

'So, as I was saying, by the words "them, or it," I meant that it depends upon the choice of the person; whether he or she gives you one of their Supporters or if they're willing to leave them both in your custody. You can also inherit just one Supporter if the other is somehow destroyed, or unable to present itself to you. If you're inheriting something, you'll feel in your heart that the Supporters are close to you. Then, you'll recognize and claim them, if the Supporters are being assigned to someone for the first time. If the person in possession of the Supporters is alive, they will know that their death is close and they will present their Supporters to you.'

Alex was amazed. This was a lot to fit in his mind. He had to remember and repeat what Mr Brown had said, again and again. Only then was he able to comprehend it. Even Vishwaroopaha, who had said some *ribtingling* things at Wasor might've gone a bit easy on Alex and his friends. He could've described things in a more complicated way. Sternind's facts were really hard to handle, indeed.

Alex stayed unmoving and silent for a long time, trying to understand what Mr Brown had said. To Mr Brown, this was supposedly all normal, as he looked in a good and *ready-to-answer-questions* mood, while quietly humming *Never gonna give you up* by Rick Astley.

Soon, Alex finished his food. Mr Brown had his meals too—Bacon, scrambled eggs and a little chocolate statue of Abraham Lincoln, which vaguely reminded Alex of the time he had been turned into a miniature black marble statue.

Alex just stood there, leaning against the glass walls of the capsule, unbothered. He looked at the amazing scenery, recapping all that had happened. The thing that caught his attention the most was what must be happening in Florida right then, and how he could handle it while being herein Sternind– believing in a "Realm" concept that was known by no one, or at least no local on Earth. He was stunned by his own thoughts. His brain had actually started to believe this seemingly trash concept, thinking that *A part of this planet is not Earth.* It was not illogical, still it was pointless. He was in a dilemma; his thoughts split between the point of view of an Earth resident and a Sternindian. It felt as if somebody was dividing his conscience and thoughts into two parts. What he needed was rest—A lot of it. But he was worried about what his adult self might be doing in Florida right then too. These were more *brain-splitting* thoughts.

He decided to first meet his friends at Mr Brown's house and tell them about what he had been thinking, about what he had seen and understood in his tour around one of Sternind's "Prants". He said to Mr Brown, 'Could you please steer us back to the restaurant? Let's get back to your house, we need to discuss all this with my friends too.'

'Okay,' Mr Brown replied as he handed some bronze coins to another robotic arm which came out of thin glass walls of the capsule, after Mr Brown summoned it with Realm Power.

Soon, Alex was inside Mr Brown's house lawn. He went inside. He found Lester and Angelina relaxing on a glass sofa, laughing while watching some kind of comedy show, that looked like Charlie Chaplin, only coloured. Alex knew for sure that it wasn't Mr Bean. He used to watch that a lot.

Alex cleared his throat to catch their attention and said, 'Ahem, Mr Brown and I are here with some important matters to discuss. Hope you both wouldn't mind if we settle ourselves on the sofas and have a word or two?'

'We won't mind, really,' Lester said, with a hint of a sarcastic tone in his voice. As Alex and Mr Brown got seated, Angelina turned off the television. She had finally learned how to use the remote controller. At least the concept wasn't *remotely* weird in its own unique way.

Alex told them about all that he had seen while he was out and what he had understood by the things Mr Brown had said. Meanwhile, Mr Brown prepared himself a cup of Liquechloro, and served some leftover cake and pizza to Lester and Angelina, occasionally adding really unhelpful comments. When Alex was talking about the Supporters' concept he started talking out of context, 'You know, I love Rick Astley's albums. Taylor Swift's songs aren't bad though... But I guess there's no comparison, is there?'

As Alex was finished, he prepared himself to answer questions that his friends would ask him. Instead, Lester said, 'Well, then. We'll talk tomorrow. You've filled me up with the news. So, thanks. By the way, I'm gonna get some sleep and use my CY device. I hope there's a room ready for me upstairs, Mr Brown. Isn't it?'

'Of course it is,' Mr Brown replied with a smile.

Lester went off to the first floor. Angelina followed him, after saying "Good night" to Alex and Mr Brown.

'You know I wanted to talk to you about something in the restaurant, right?' Alex asked Mr Brown.

'I do remember that, and I also remember that you forgot to mention the main purpose of our visit there.'

'It was about *why us*? Why did Vishwaroopaha say

that we were chosen to be among "them"? Who are "them", though? The Sternindians?,' Alex said, using air quotes.

'Yeah, I was wanting you to talk about that. I was out of my mind wondering why hasn't any of you asked me about one of the most… What's the word… Ah, intriguing things said to you all..'

'Yeah, so now do me a favour and cough up the whole "being chosen" thing.'

'Later, boy. Later. You're not getting any answers right now.'

Annoyed, Alex started walking upstairs, too, but Mr Brown interrupted him, 'I'm afraid we'll have to sleep here. There's no room for us upstairs.'

'Here? On these see-through sofas?'

'Oh, you see, they are transparent now, like glass. If I concentrate, I can make them any colour or cushion-type. These house decorations depend on the owner's mood. Which colour do you need to sleep on today?'

Alex wasn't so excited with the colour-changing idea, but he settled on his favourite colour. 'Let's go with blue.'

Immediately, as Mr Brown closed his eyes, the soft and cushiony sofas turned into different elegant shades of blue.

Alex relaxed himself, lay on the sofa, and took out the CY device from his pocket. Surprisingly, it was there. Alex hadn't expected that. He'd thought that Mr Brown must have hidden it somewhere after using some spell to change Alex and his friends' clothes, but it was still in his pocket. He sat up straight to ask Mr Brown whether he too had experienced something like these CY devices earlier. But Alex couldn't find him in the living room. Mr Brown might've had his instincts about Alex asking him more questions, so he'd probably set off.

Alex fiddled with the CY device in his hands, carefully looking at it from every angle, trying to figure out what was special about it.

On the surface of the CY device, opposite to the screen, there inscribed was a familiar symbol which Alex recognized.

It was the same symbol he had seen during his survey of the mansion at Wasor Island; it was perfectly carved into a wall. It was no doubt the same weird symbol.

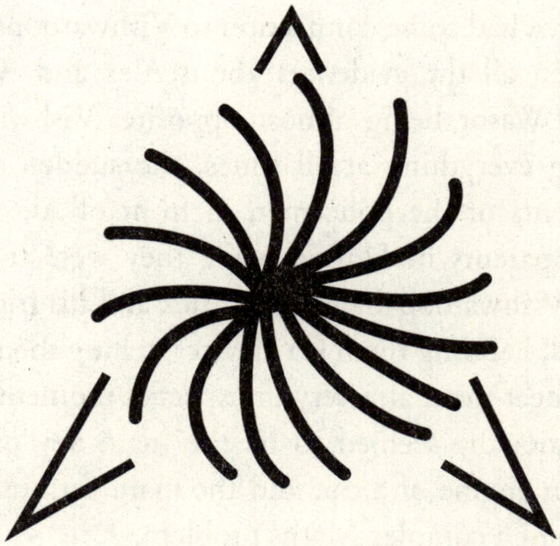

This raised a question in Alex's mind. Vishwaroopaha had given him the device with this symbol on it, hinting that it somehow belonged to him. The same symbol was on the walls in the mansion. Then... Was it possible that the mansion had also been his property...? Or worse... Had he *made* these CY devices? If yes, then he had to have made that mansion. If this was the truth, then, in the worst case scenario, Vishwaroopaha might've *made* Wasor Island... But, that couldn't be true. Even with his "Realm Power", he couldn't have intended to kill Alex and his friends and get away with making such a big landmass. But that was possible somehow, as he was a stranger to Alex and his friends till then, and they didn't know much about him. Mr Brown was a stranger, too. Alex didn't like being in the company of such unpredictable people. All in all, what he learned from these thoughts was that this CY device had some connection to Vishwaroopaha.

Given all the evidences about Alex and Angelina's tasks at Wasor being almost opposite, Vishwaroopaha knowing everything at all times, the sudden shocking movements of the policemen in front of Alex and his friends' parents in Florida while they were trapped at Wasor, Vishwaroopaha sending Alex and his friends to a Sternind, handing them CY devices, telling them that he would meet them at a very unexpected moment... Here, Vishwaroopaha seemed to be the main key of a lock, the main engine of a car, and the main formula for the solution of a complex Maths problem.

To get some positive inputs on his theory, Alex truly

needed someone to be there and reaffirm his thoughts. But he put those doubts aside for later, and decided to keep himself busy, and invest an hour in trying out his CY device.

He switched it on by pressing the button at its side. Suddenly, a man looking as if he was going through his late twenties appeared on the screen, standing on an invisible ground with a white background screen behind him. He wore a circus joker's outfit.

He said, 'Hi. I'll be your Control Yourself assistant. A digital minion, with a mind of its own! Please speak out loud what language you'll be conversing in with me.' He started repeating this in many other languages Alex didn't understand.

'English,' Alex replied.

'May I know your name so that I can find your account and sync your data with this device?'

'Alex Drake.'

'Password?'

Alex decided hit-and-trial. Maybe Vishwaroopaha had created an account for him with an easy-to-guess password. 'Wasor,' Alex said.

'Very well,' the minion said. 'Hello. I'm your assistant Alexander the Great. Please tell me in what mode would you like to operate your clone—Automatic or Manual?'

Alex gaped at the awkwardness of this CY device. Who could possibly name a personal assistant Alexander the Great?

'Difference between the two?'

'In automatic mode, you'll have to gain my support by being my friend, and I'll do all the work you tell me to do through the clone. In manual mode, you'll have to operate a touchpad, a command box, a speech box, and many movement controls all by yourself. I'll not be there to aid you. If you ask me, that's a total waste of time. A lot of hard work is needed. But yes, if you opt for automatic mode, you can supervise over me.'

'First of all, change into a more formal and better dress. Let's go with automatic mode, and mind yourself, don't do anything unless I tell you to.'

Alexander's appearance changed. He was now wearing a plain black shirt with white pants. 'I may or may not do what you tell me to do. That's why I was asking you to do me a favour. If you don't, then I'll make sure I damage your rep using your clone. I am in control of you on Earth, don't forget that.' He smiled mischievously.

Alex was really annoyed. The last thing he needed to do was some more important *key-to-success* work.

'What favour do you want in exchange for your loyal service?' Alex demanded from Alexander.

'Oh, nothing. Just a few digital CY decoration packs worth only 20 Dinks. Let's go to the market.'

Alex didn't get what those words meant. Maybe "Dinks" was the currency of Sternind. This was too much for Alex to handle, so he said to Alexander, 'It's pretty late right now. I'll ask Mr Brown to buy them for you tomorrow when I go out to get my Supporters. So right now, shut up.' Alex switched off the device before

Alexander had a chance to reply.

Alex closed his eyes and decided to take some rest, trying not to care about anything. He shut his mind, and drifted into peaceful sleep. At least there were no dreams like the warning dream at Wasor Island.

Chapter 5

A *Lovely* Little Excursion to *Friendly* Outer Space

Alex woke up and found Mr Brown leaning over him, observing his face carefully as if he were a thing Mr Brown had discovered after eons of searching. With a disgusted expression on his face, Alex pushed Mr Brown away and stood up next to him as he straightened himself. Without giving Mr Brown any opportunity to blabber more things about Sternind, Alex said, 'Good morning' and raced towards the main lawn. Lester and Angelina were on the lawn like the previous night, and they were doing what they were doing the previous night—Talking. The scene looked so familiar and upsetting that Alex wanted to... Forget it. Why the hell had all this happened?

Alex waved the thought aside and sat down next to Angelina, waiting for someone to say something. But both his friends stopped their conversation immediately and started staring into the open sky, no doubt wondering many things, feeling helpless from inside. Alex broke the silence, saying, 'So, what are our plans for the day? Wanna head to *The Walking Talks*?'

Lester replied lazily, 'No, I don't think I care about some fancy restaurant. But what bothered me the most last night was that… thing about those *Supporters*. I really need something to get interesting in my life...' His face lit up mid-sentence. He stood up and said, turning his tone from lazy to cheerful, 'Let's go get our Supporters!'

'Of course we'll do that. Also today, you'll all see Alex's petty wish being fulfilled and will get admission in SIRP. I had promised Veshverupeha to get you three just one night's stay at my house. Tonight, you'll all find yourselves in SIRP's respective dorms, unless any of you dies because of brain haemorrhage during the tests of your imagination,' Mr Brown added. He was dressed in a maroon and white outfit, and decently polished black shoes. His hair was neatly combed and his eyepatch looked like a pirate's.

Which petty wish? Alex thought, but decided to bring it up later, and first see how things unfold. All he knew was that it could later turn out to be some joke, so he decided to not pay much attention to it right then.

He was really fed up with Mr Brown's habit of pronouncing Vishwaroopaha's name incorrectly and his *scaring-to-death* warnings. He decided to tolerate it anyway.

As they set off, following Mr Brown, Alex started increasing his pace. He walked up to Mr Brown and asked curiously, 'What are Dinks?'

'Oh, of course, Dink is the currency of Sternind.'

'Right.'

Alex decided not to ask anything else, for Mr Brown was surely going to explain a lot of Sternind's "facts" that day.

During the day, the streets were packed with more people and their Supporters, but Alex decided not to pay attention to the surroundings much. He wondered what his friends' reaction was when they first saw the world of Sternind with their own eyes, but just by looking at them, he got his answer. They were *oohing* and *aahing* continuously, as Mr Brown commented on the beauty of the surroundings.

Alex was wondering about many things when he heard Mr Brown muttering, 'There we are. Off you go, children.'

Alex started hating being referred to as "Children" along with his friends, but he knew he had to get used to it. The shop's title board said –

Snowy Supporters

GET `EM
OR INHERIT `EM AT LEAST
OR U AIN'T
LEAVIN' IN ONE PIECE

Alex was intrigued by the death threat of the shop, though he did not feel threatened. He went in through the door, followed by the rest. Inside was a vast *outdoor*, endless grassland. There was no roof, even though the place appeared closed from the outside. The sun shone brightly overhead. Droplets of sweat ran down Alex's cheeks.

'What is this?' Lester asked, seemingly in awe. '*This* is what you call *snowy* in Sternind?'

'Hmm...' Mr Brown replied with a thoughtful look on his face. 'There used to be a *plummet-to-death* ice skating rink here to test you if you were worthy of possessing newly assigned Supporters, but now... It seems as if it's been moved somewhere or... They've made it easy, *specifically* for you all. You need to get through the test by locating a place where you can get your Supporters. There isn't an instruction board around to help you locate the shop, but... If I were you, I would have done an obvious act of getting to it somehow. If you use your imagination in trying to find it, I think it will show up. Always remember that your imagination is very powerful. It can lead you from a state of anxiety to total depression. Sternind is all about creative imagination. You just need to be imaginative.'

'So... What imagination? How do we *use* it?' Angelina said.

'It's all inside you. You are the one that has to figure out the way Realm Power works. The hint is already given—Imagination.'

Mr Brown went off towards a different spot of the far-flung and seemingly never-ending grassland and began refuelling his Aviaboards while they were in key shape. He started doing hand-movements around them, like how Alex thought most usage of Realm Power in Sternind was typically done. Orange and black fumes originated from the tips of his fingers and solidified on the keys, being absorbed by the metal the very next second.

Alex wondered where Mr Brown had headed off to the previous night. If he was refuelling them right then, it meant that he had obviously travelled somewhere at night. He was waving his hands around *all* the keys, which made Alex suspicious about why the Aviaboards need refuelling. He abruptly stopped thinking about all this and concentrated on finding the shop through his imagination.

He closed his eyes and imagined plotting his surroundings against a Three Dimensional software's measuring grid. He scaled on to the isometric view and began scanning the long expanse of land in front of him in a computer-like manner in his mind. He knew that it was his imagination and he wouldn't find anything new that his mind hadn't made up while he was imaginatively scanning the grassland as far as the eye could see.

But to his astonishment, he found a small wooden hut, on which there was a label—Snowy Supporters. He believed that this was his imagination too, but he decided it was worth checking out. He measured the distance between him and the hut in his imagined 3-D software and found it to be five hundred meters. He opened his eyes and decided to head there, gesturing his confused looking friends to follow him.

Alex didn't bother leaving Mr Brown behind, for he could take care of himself pretty well. Alex moved towards the hut and found it in reality. Rubbing his eyes to make himself believe that he had passed the test, he smiled.

Alex went in and found himself with his friends overlooking a cold and high-rise snowy mountain landscape. 'The name still fits for this place, after all,' Alex said. He glanced down and yelped. One more step and they could've plummeted down to a snowy death.

It was confusing how a street shop could host a large grassland, and another shop inside the grassland could hold an entire mountain range with cold winds blowing everywhere. But then, Sternind was all about overcoming science concepts.

'*That* was close,' Angelina exclaimed as she pointed towards the *likely-to-plummet* snowy valley.

'Yup,' Lester said in agreement. 'This could be the ice skating rink Mr Brown mentioned. But I see no one... What should we do?'

'I think...' Alex said, 'We need to search for something in order to continue. The test is still going on.'

'It's not,' a booming male voice echoed in the snowy hills. 'Congratulations, the three of you have proved yourselves worthy of having Supporters. You are inheriting Articles of Power, but none of you is being assigned Majenimals, keeping your educational qualifications in consideration. They may be assigned after a specific time period of receiving education in SIRP.'

Three wooden structures solidified in the air before

them, green mist swirling around each one. Angelina's Article of Power was an eagle perched over a wooden stick. Lester's AOP had a miniature statue of someone holding a book. Alex had inherited some sort of a wooden hand on a stick which was a bit scratched at the tip of the index finger.

'That's it?' Alex said in awe. 'No more tests? Mr Brown had been going on and on about dangers... Is it so easy?'

'I think, yes, it is,' Angelina said convincingly. 'We *have already been through* the tests. I think Vishwaroopaha more or less got us a free ticket for getting Supporters by maybe mentioning our experience at Wasor Island to whoever manages all this stuff. Plus, we can say that locating this place was also a test.'

'Right,' Lester nodded in agreement, smiling in a somewhat weird way. 'For now, let's get going on our trip to fulfil Alex's *petty wish*. Do you even know what it is, Alex?' He made a face at Alex, but Alex didn't react.

As they reached Mr Brown in the grassland, he perked up. A smile of admiration spread across his face. Now Alex had two strangely smiling people with him. 'By golly, is... Is that a copy of the Primo?' Mr Brown said as he gestured towards Alex. 'Oh my... Haven't seen one in years...'

Mr Brown didn't seem fazed about their early return, so Alex guessed he might know about Wasor Island. As Mr Brown was so excited to see a *wooden hand*, Alex replied with an **I-don't-care-what-this-is-but-whatever-this-is-I-will-keep-**

it look, 'I don't know what that is... Can you please fill me in?'

'Ahem,' Mr Brown replied, 'This is a copy of the most responding and trusting AOP known till date, the Primo. No one knows even if it's real or is just a rumour, but people like imagining what it might've been like and try to make it somewhat like the rumoured AOP. You see, the hand on it? It's the center of power and learning. A commendable symbolic representation, it is. Good, you'll catch up with it, Alex.'

'Gee, thanks.' Alex had become so used to Mr Brown's long and complicated lectures that he had lost interest in them. But he decided to move on, keeping the information in some corner of his mind, intuiting that he would need it later.

By the looks of her face, Angelina got excited by just listening to Mr Brown about AOPs. She asked anxiously, 'What does this eagle mean on my AOP?'

Mr Brown explained that the eagle was named Flyoid and helped with a sense of sharp eyesight, and the ability to... Blah Blah Blah. Alex didn't really care, but listened to what Mr Brown was saying.

The man holding a book on Lester's AOP was looking much like Mr Brown holding the book labelled GUIDE (which he never read) close to his chest. Mr Brown explained that it was a symbol of knowledge and enlightenment. It was commonly called Cruxstrategio.

Alex figured Mr Brown would talk endlessly about the applications and features of the AOPs, so he gestured towards an exit door within sight and shouted, knowing perfectly well that no one would hear him except Mr Brown, Lester and Angelina, 'I'm going ahead. Anyone wanna come, or shall I prepare to spend the whole day picking grass?'

The three of them came after him, still talking about their AOPs. 'So,' Mr Brown said as all four of them started again on the footpath, 'Now, let's get to the Sternindian space observatory. It's time for your petty wish, Alex. I hope you survive.'

Alex's heart crawled up into his throat. He had been dreading this moment, when the center of attraction, or *center of distraction* was him. Instead of getting to SIRP, they were on a little detour which Alex was not likely to *survive...*?

There were many questions in Alex's mind. As much as he recalled, he had never made a wish involving a space observatory. He really didn't remember what his "Petty Wish" had been. Moreover, he wasn't keen to be floating in space in an underprotected shuttle, or worse. 'What wish is it…?' he asked Mr Brown. 'Could you *please* tell that now? I mean, we've got the idea of what is Sternind and all that's happening, so why conceal anything from us now?'

Mr Brown laughed. 'You don't even know a little about Sternind yet, m'boy. If judging by Earth's standards, it's like you've learned ABCD, framing sentences, and numbers from one to fifty in school and you claim that you have practiced Calculus for quite a long time,' he said. Alex got his reply. There was simply *too* much to learn. He decided to stay quiet.

Soon they reached what *didn't* look like a space observatory. 'We're here,' Mr Brown said. There wasn't a building campus, neither a signboard saying *Sternind Space Observatory*. There was just a large cuboidal vertical tunnel leading somewhere higher than clouds. There was a large uninhabited colony of red tall buildings at the base of the *elevator-like-vertical-in-air-passageway*, surrounded by a really big crowd of people spread around. It was hard to look at the place without any interruption. Alex could only make out red stone and high-rise buildings.

Mr Brown might've figured they needed some explanation, so he launched into a lecture, 'You see, by overcoming science concepts, we have made a building that is on Sternind but is as high up as the space. This vertical passageway has an elevator which takes us above Sternind's atmosphere, and gives the Sternindians a full view of the space nearby. No need to carry out a mission to send a *satellite* or spacecraft to some planet, just zoom in and you've got a high-resolution image provided to you by insanely powerful cameras. Now you'd be wondering how is such a tower made? First, by using Realm Power and proving science concepts wrong. Second, by providing a broad base to the structure to reduce pressure on the ground. The red high-rise uninhabited building you see is the broad base. The rest is managed by Realm Power. Everything is constructed intricately, even the support of such a tall structure at its base. Everything in Sternind is precious, and the base of the only Space observatory in Sternind is a major tourist attraction, much like all the tourists of the seven wonders of Earth are together to view the base. Only authorized personnel and their guests are allowed inside the observatory, but no need to worry. I'm the guy you need.'

As Alex learned all this, surprisingly, no questions popped up in his mind. He was finally starting to understand that something *could* prove that science can be wrong. Sternind was a place where things were awkward *and* amazing.

He decided to get to the observatory and check out the cool stuff, but the words *outer space* reminded him of something. Just as Mr Brown talked more about the Space Observatory while he showed his authorization card to the lift attendant and the elevator lurched upward carrying the four of them, Alex recalled a quite hazy memory of his petty wish.

By the time the elevator's doors opened, he remembered what his petty wish was. It wasn't the kind in which he would suffer less or no harm; it was very different. He had truly made a petty wish while lamenting his ill-luck at Wasor, 'Rather than witnessing all this stuff, I'd love to be lost in endless space!' Alex decided to excuse himself and his friends from Mr Brown to inform them about it but the view of the observatory made Alex forget all that—momentarily.

Just as the elevator doors parted, they found themselves in a cuboidal glass-walled room, with a lot of large telescopes sticking out of them into space. There were many scientists (*or whatever Sternindian Scientists are known as*, Alex thought) involved in research. They were doing some work or the other, such as using telescopes, or studying some maps. There were some tourists (*or whatever Authorised Personnel in such a place are known as*, Alex thought) that were looking at the beauty of space. There were labels on the glass walls to indicate an attraction. Alex froze in his tracks just by the view. Lester and Angelina started making really positive comments right away. Mr Brown occasionally agreed by saying, 'Yes! That's how cool it is!' or 'You're right, man. Isn't this interesting?'

What caught Alex's attention was the thought about what was going to happen due to his "petty wish". But Mr Brown must have got the hint that Alex was up to something, so he distracted Alex by taking him and his friends to a spot that read **The Fusionotica Experience**. There was another smaller label just a little lower than the heading which read MOST POPULAR in red ink.

Alex was excited. He went up there first and peeped through the small hole Mr Brown had instructed him to look through. He saw a partial Earth's landmass and partial Sternind's landmass fused into one planet. Earth was the same as seen by Earth's satellites' views, but Sternind, not being a shade of green and blue, was white in the middle, brown in the region surrounding it and the rest of Sternind's land was green and dark blue coloured. Alex doubted that this was real. It seemed so real to him that– Suddenly, as he was thinking all this, someone bumped his right arm, and thus his vision through the telescope changed as his eyes tilted a little towards left. The view changed. Now, he noticed the whole of Sternind as a planet. As he drifted right, he observed the Earth as a whole planet. In the middle view, they could be seen partially on the right and left halves. This proved that the theory of different dimensions of the same planet was true. The fact that one could see both the dimensions using Realm Power while being *on* one of them was spellbinding.

Alex's admiration filled thoughts were interrupted when something shook behind him, and the floor where he'd been standing broke apart from the observatory. Since the Sternindians had overcome science concepts, there appeared no change in their observatory as Alex got separated from it. For some reason vacuum did not take hold of the people inside the observatory, and everything looked fine inside, even when the ground had broken apart, taking the telescope and glass panes with it. Alex's fears had come true. Standing beside him on the piece of cemented floor were his friends, looking shocked and rattled. Mr Brown, while being safe in the miraculous observatory was waving his hands towards them, as if saying bye forever. Alex registered this scene in his mind, not caring about how the people in the observatory would react if they found out that Mr Brown had attempted to murder or send him and his friends to a one-way trip to outer space. He saw broken pieces of glass and stone floating with him and his friends in space.

Alex had just enough time to understand that Mr Brown had done all this, when his vision blurred, his intestines churned, and he felt like he was lying in a place a million times colder than a freezer. He decided he could do nothing about it, and broke down mentally, giving up hope of life. This time, there was really no way that he and his friends would live.

Suddenly, time seemed to slow down, and Alex realized it was his mind shutting. But as it turned out, it wasn't what he thought it was.

Angelina's AOP started shaking. Alex looked down at his Supporter and found it shaking too. Lester's AOP was doing the same. Alex interpreted this as some kind of warning that the AOPs were ready to get inherited by someone else, saying their goodbye to him and his friends while they were dying.

Again, Alex was proved wrong. Suddenly, the eyes of Angelina's AOP's eagle, the eyes of the man depicted on Lester's AOP, and Alex's AOP's sculpted hand's fingertips started glowing red. The red light from all three AOPs floated in front of Alex to form a red ball and then exploded, blinding him.

When Alex's vision cleared, he found him and his friends being rapidly hauled towards the observatory and the pieces of glass and stone that had been shattered, were joining again. Everything was put back, as if someone had just reversed time. In not more than two seconds, Alex found himself breathing heavily in a corner of the observatory, his friends at his side. He was elated, but worn out and on the verge of having a mental breakdown. He collapsed and lost consciousness.

Alex came to after what seemed like ages. 'How… How long have I been passed out…?' he asked Lester as he stood up, who was looking a bit dazed. 'Not more than two seconds,' Mr Brown's casual voice replied from behind Lester. Alex was amazed, but was *I'm-gonna-kill-you-right-away* level angry with Mr Brown.

He stormed towards the source of the voice. Mr Brown raised his hands in surrender. 'Can we talk peacefully somewhere? I really don't want you guys mad at me again.'

'Fine,' Alex replied grudgingly.

Soon, Alex found himself out of the observatory, heading towards a cafe titled THE CHEAPY CAFÉ. He didn't bother to ponder over the name, as he headed straight in and ordered a Latte. The shopkeeper seemed confused by his order, which Alex guessed was obvious. '*Coforette*,' Mr Brown corrected. Alex stared at the awkwardness. But all this had started becoming familiar to him by then.

'So,' Alex said as all four of them settled around a table. 'First of all, tell us that what was *Nerdhlic Hagcne* that Vishwaroopaha had instructed you to do. Was it Sternindian language?'

Mr Brown laughed. 'It was nothing. Just scrambled

letters for the words "Children Change", and that's what happened to you three. Mission accomplished! Of course it's not permissible in this Prant, but exceptions can be made, can't they?' He smiled and continued, 'And, as for Sternindian language, there's no particular language spoken in Sternind. Converse in any language you want, as long as the person whom you're talking to understands it clearly. The most common languages used are English, French, Spanish, Sanskrit and Hindi.'

'Hindi?'

'You know, the official language of India.'

Alex received few answers but then asked, 'Okay, I've tolerated enough. I want to know your main motive– first getting us in Sternind, liquefying us, and then freaking *dispatching us into space*. Just don't throw *fate*, *coincidence*, or *petty wish* in my face. I want the answer—Fair and Square. Unless you want three people to…' he faltered, not sure how he could beat Mr Brown in *anything*.

'Yup. I want to know that too. Fair and square,' Lester stated, seconding what Alex had said.

'Mmm… Yeah, fair and square,' Angelina agreed in a muffled voice, with a grilled sandwich stuffed in her mouth. *At least there isn't another name for that in Sternind*, Alex thought.

'I… I'm surprised to be treated like this… Bu–'

Alex flared up. 'So how should we treat you? Talk to you with prefixes like "Your Highness"?'

'I would appreciate that, but no, thank you,' Mr Brown replied sarcastically. 'I'm afraid your queries will have to wait for the next twelve hours. I bet you'll be really touched when you get the answers to all of them. I'm not actually refusing to get on with your questions, but I think the reason for you guys getting lost in space – even though for a very short time – was clear to you. You all really need to get through a lot of tests to become a qualified member of Sternind, in most of which there are very high chances of dying. I confess, I was *not* going to get you guys out of it, even if you were not saved by your Articles Of Power. You all are very lucky to not have suffered serious injuries or death by now. It is all about your imagination in Sternind.'

Mr Brown changed his tone by the look of Alex's expression. 'Now, you guys might be thinking that I'm drifting off the topic, but I'm assuring you all this is connected. Just don't think about the "Being lost in Space" thing, as it wasn't betrayal *at all*. It's wrong, all that's happening to you all, but sometimes in life you just need to go through moments like these. Remember, good days are about to come. Everything regarding your tests – unrelated to SIRP – is over now. Sternind Institute of Realm Power learning is gonna be superb. You'll forget all that's happened to you when you get there.'

Alex understood that Mr Brown won't slip up information anymore. That was his final word. And Alex didn't insist, as he didn't want to get physical.

'Off we go, now,' announced Mr Brown as the four of them finished their break and set out on the footpath again. 'Behold, SIRP, here we come!'

Chapter 6

Sternind Institute of Realm Power learning

Before even hearing the name of Sternind Institute of Realm Power learning, Alex had wondered what SIRP would look like. What would it be about? What all would he experience there? He just hoped that it wasn't a type of a school where kids ran around with superpowers. But, by then, everything—Sternind, the life-and-death situations, Sternind's streets, and all of this unusual stuff had become familiar to him. He would have to get used to that too.

'Ah, and I must clarify one thing, which most of the Freshers always misunderstand,' Mr Brown said, completely out of the blue. He didn't usually say much while they were on the footpath, which Alex guessed was because of his concentration on framing his sentences – one needs a lot of control over words to extemporarily explain concepts like Mr Brown – or simply his lack of interest. 'This is a very common misunderstanding, so listen carefully—This is *not* a wizarding world. We aren't witches or wizards. We are Sternindians. We don't need a stick – or a wand, as it is so called – and utter stupid *spells*, to perform *magic*. In Sternind, we don't perform magic, we make use of the power – Realm Power – that the Realms hold. We don't have to open our mouth to do wonders using Realm Power; not at all waste our energy in saying some *abracadabra*. We just need to let our imagination believe that the sky is the limit, and that's just a phrase. After all, as we need some support in life, we need Supporters. So don't mistake them for wands. I gotta warn you all, *don't* think of Realm Power as magic,' he said as he suddenly leaned down towards the three of them. He hushed his tone, and continued, 'Pro tip: You know what, in Sternind, *magician* is referred to as the worst insult or abuse possible. It's almost like you're saying the N-word. That's why I wanted to be transparent about this stuff.'

Just as he completed that sentence, a lot of questions departed into oblivion from Alex's mind. He noticed that some of the tension on Lester and Angelina's face was also drained. Sure, there were still many questions, but a little sense of confusion had been erased by then.

Alex had another bunch of queries in mind, all related to a particular topic. So he decided to loosen the knot of the anxiety in his mind by asking Mr Brown, 'I just really don't understand it. You say, there is an institute for making people learn Realm Power. Wouldn't it be a since-birth quality of Sternind-born people to have known how to make use of it? If yes, then you – by whom I mean experienced Sternindians – might be teaching "New Sternindian Freshers" in SIRP, just like us, who have arrived here from Earth. If it's not a since-birth quality, then you might be teaching both Sternindians, Earth's inhabitants, and *former* Earth's inhabitants in SIRP. If that is not so, then you might be educating only Sternindians in SIRP. If that is so, then I need to ask, why are we the only children from Earth to ever arrive in Sternind? If it is not so, then I want to ask how do you get these "New Sternindian Freshers" to be here? By leaving their lives on Earth? Do they even live in Sternind forever? Is there some mailing system to invite them to Sternind, or what…?' Alex poured out all his questions related to the topic.

'Whoa, man,' Lester said, his eyes widening. 'How long have you been thinking about this?'

Mr Brown chuckled. 'That is a large volley of queries and… Well, something which I would term as, *mid-question-conclusions*. I am really impressed by these questions. Nobody has ever been able to grasp the concepts and come up with so many ifs and buts in such a short time,' he said, adding, 'At least none that I know of.'

'Boy, you know, everyone deserves to have a bit of mystery and *paranormality* in their lives,' Mr Brown started with a quick glance towards Alex. 'The Freshers aren't chosen, rather the common people living on Earth are provided secret clues, which they need to identify.

They need to solve the mystery, explore the secret concept of Sternind, make reasonable choices, and then become a Sternindian. All we need is another dimension of the planet, better and more prosperous in knowledge and common sense than Earth. If not a mystery, then many people are invited to Sternind just like you, keeping in account that they have faced adventures – not solved mysteries – earlier. Your adventures were at Wasor Island. But there's still something special about you guys. Every Fresher doesn't get a privilege to have an *all-you-need-to-know* guide like me with them. They all are handed some cheap brochures and the guide book you had seen me holding yesterday night.'

Lester spat some *Coforette* from his mouth. He was walking with a cup in his hand. 'You mean we could have avoided you if we had those...?' he said in disbelief.

'No,' Mr Brown smiled. 'You couldn't have got rid of me anyway.'

Lester scowled disdainfully.

'Just two more questions,' Alex said to Mr Brown, stopping Lester from saying anything more. 'Okay, this one might seem a little stupid, but… If Sternind's inhabitants are called Sternindians, then why aren't Earth's inhabitants called "Earthians" in Sternind?'

'For that,' Mr brown said, laughing softly. 'You'll need to check the GUIDE book out. I honestly have no idea. Anyway, what's the second question?'

'If some people like us do not inherit Majenimals or don't care to pick them out, or aren't given a chance to select them, when and how will they receive them later? Or *will* they?'

'That is a source of concern, I agree,' Mr Brown replied. But don't worry. Mentors at SIRP will let you know.'

Alex glanced at his friends just as he got his unsatisfying answer. He figured he hadn't talked to them lately. So he decided to start a conversation with Lester. Apparently Lester had been thinking the same, so he said to Alex, just loud enough for the three friends to listen, 'You really lifted a burden from my mind, buddy. I feel better. Sorry for not talking much. I was just… Confused.'

'Yeah, me too. Those sandwiches were amazing. They *did* ease me. Thank god I'm ready to talk in complete sentences again,' Angelina said, with a hint of cheer in her voice.

'I'm glad you guys have got through… this stuff. But what really troubles me is how mysterious Mr Brown is. I mean, we know little about him and he even knows about what happened at Wasor. Vishwaroopaha is an unpredictable man too, but he seemed harmless until the night when we started for Sternind. I didn't want to, but Vishwaroopaha made us go with Mr Brown, and I *had* to say yes. It doesn't matter now, but all I can say is that it was a physical threat,' replied Alex.

'What, really?' Lester said.

'These guys can do anything, man. They are… dangerous. We haven't got the knack of using Realm

Power like they do. I just hope that they don't turn into the next Cloedboriogds. No offense, Angelina.'

'None taken,' Angelina agreed as she nodded.

'For now,' Lester said with a *this-is-the-final-decision-I-hope-you-all-don't-want-to-overrule-it* tone in his voice, 'let's just act like we aren't suspicious of anything. We can't let Mr Brown doubt us.'

'I heard all that,' said Mr Brown as he turned back and approached the friends, who had now stopped talking. Alex immediately felt stupid and believed that all this hushed talking had been in vain. They stayed quiet after that, and resumed walking, while Mr Brown escorted them; a mischievous smile spread on his face.

Alex figured he needed some *brain-boosting* experience and the potential to handle what all was ahead of him. And he knew just the thing required—Relaxation and Fun. 'Can we halt for a while somewhere? Not that I am complaining I want to head for a place better than THE CHEAPY CAFÉ, but actually I just need to... Gather myself.'

'I'm afraid we are in a tight spot here,' Mr Brown replied in the same way. 'Not that I am refusing to go someplace for a short stop but... You know, I gotta give this round to the crunch of time.'

Knowing that nothing could be done now, Alex kept walking, not sure of anything. His legs started feeling wobbly, but there was a "time crunch" preventing him from resting. In order to take his mind off the pain, he tried a recapitulation of all he knew about Sternind and the "Realm" concept. He made a list in his mind –

√ "Realm" concept.
√ Dimension Name – Sternind.
Continents – ?
Countries – ?
Cities – ?
"Prants" as States.
√ Structure – As seen by the telescope from observatory.
√ People – American, British and... Indian? African?
√ Mode of transport – Majenimals
√ Supernatural Quality – "Realm Power"
On Earth, "RP"
√ "Realm Power" – Power granted to all the three realms' inhabitants by this realm–Sternind. Not found within oneself until one has been taught how to make use of it.
√ Extraordinary Objects – ~~Wands~~
~~Magical Staffs~~
AOPs (One of the Supporters)
√ Pets – ~~Cat~~
~~Dog~~
~~Owl~~
Majenimal (A Supporter)
~~Rat~~

Majenimal (A Supporter)
and
Majenimal (A Supporter)

Along with a lot more unusual **facts**...
Experience – Ghastly
Rating on Alex'sAdvice.com – 0.5/5

'Okay, that's all for now, not to mention the CY devices, precise definition of Supporters, blah blah blah,' Alex said to himself, wondering if he was giving way too much thought to all this.

Remembering the CY device, he told Mr Brown what Alexander had asked for the night before. He mentioned its price—20 Dinks. Mr Brown nodded and fetched a piece of plastic with a rectangular piece of metal jutting out of its one end – a pen drive – from a nearby shop. Or that was what Alex thought of it as, anyway. 'Insert this in a socket in your CY device. Just do what I say, Alexander will be happy,' Mr Brown said as he rushed back to the shop and started buying the accessories Lester and Angelina's CY devices needed.

Alex figured Mr Brown wasn't really against them, since he was buying things for them. But Vishwaroopaha might've provided the money for that, since he had given them the CY devices in the first place.

Alex knew he wasn't potent enough to handle Alexander and his attitude at the moment, so he put the piece of plastic in his pocket. But Lester and Angelina started having fun with their virtual friends and got busy controlling their clones right away, even while walking.

A while later, as Angelina and Lester put the CY devices back into their pockets, Mr Brown indicated that they'd arrived. 'So,' he said, gesturing towards a structure on the right side of the footpath, 'what do you all see? You might be wondering why I'm asking this question. It's just because what you might be seeing isn't what others are seeing. Many people interpret SIRP in different ways. That's just the nature of their imagination. SIRP is a white, tall building, but you three might be seeing it differently, as you all haven't tamed your imagination. Now, just tell me what you see.'

Alex saw a white, tall building, just as Mr Brown had said. He also observed the same symbol on the white wall which he had found on the back of his CY device and in the mansion at Wasor. That surely meant that the symbol was of SIRP. Also, Alex was relieved that his imagination was tame. But one thing was different from Mr Brown's description. Alex also noticed a faint green aura glowing around the building. He told everyone what he perceived. Mr Brown didn't react, rather asked Angelina about what she was looking at.

'I see a grand castle, full of guards and royal rooms. Isn't that a positive sign?' Angelina said.

'I'm afraid it isn't, Angelina,' Mr Brown replied. 'This just means that in order to see SIRP clearly, you'll have to get in the castle by the front door, then through the castle's guards and king, and finally reach the back door, which you'll later perceive as the main door of SIRP. This is a quest. I say this from personal experience, since it looked like a castle to me, too. Okay, so I just told you what you'll have to do. Now, go. It's going to be hard.'

Angelina headed in through the front door of the white building, or at least that was what Alex thought of it. To Angelina, it was a castle. 'What do you see, Lester?' Mr Brown asked.

Lester whimpered. 'You know I'm acrophobic. And much to my freakin' disappointment, I see a car, a road that rises high into the clouds, and... Oh no, no– no. I'm– I'm dead. I ain't doing this. Uh, Mr Brown, is it possible for me to *not* get to SIRP? I know this might sound weird, but… You know, I guess I'll just wait right here until Angelina and Alex are done with their tests.'

'And then? You're gonna wait another six years?' Alex said.

'That is not possible, Lester,' Mr Brown replied. 'You can't do that, and we all know why. Just overcome your fear. Six years is a long time. After all, look on the bright side—You're getting to drive a car at the age of fourteen!'

'I've already driven a car,' Lester said sheepishly, and continued to grumble some unpleasant words, whilst moving towards the thing which Alex saw as the door of SIRP, but to Lester... It might've been different. The door of the car he was going to drive, maybe?

'What should *I* do now?' Alex asked Mr Brown. 'Get in through the door?'

'No. It has been a long time since somebody looked

at SIRP in its original form, without getting through any obstacle. You are special, Alex. I think the… uhh, *adventures* you had faced might've been very hard to get through. You just need to wait until your friends get past their hurdles, which usually takes about an hour. We must lounge about in another restaurant. I think you can finally get the rest you had been longing.'

'But I need to aid my friends,' Alex protested.

'No, it's *their* work. They have to do it individually.'

Alex spotted a place titled SIRP CAFÉ – BY FRESHERS, FOR FRESHERS. But he decided not to go there, noticing a change in his mood. He'd had enough of new places and people. He didn't even feel like asking anything else. He didn't want to use his CY device. He just needed a place to get the stress off of him. He wanted to be away from Mr Brown, just with his friends, crack a joke or two, and then take a quick nap. Unfortunately, that wasn't possible at that time.

Suddenly, he heard a whooshing sound behind him. He thought it might've been a Majenimal racing past. But, that was where Mr Brown was standing. As he heard Mr Brown's scream, the incident made sense. He just had the time to think, 'Uh-oh' as he turned, and found a blood-soaked Mr Brown lying on the road, curled up like a ball. His dress was tattered, and he wasn't moving at all. But, his rapid breathing indicated that at least he was alive.

Alex rushed to help Mr Brown, not thinking twice. All he cared about was being humane, regardless of what Mr Brown had done to him and his friends. He was helped by some kind strangers as he tried to carry Mr Brown. 'There,' Alex said to the people holding Mr Brown. 'Let's get him to the *SIRP Café* nearby. We might get some first aid.' The strangers seemed confused, but nodded.

As they hauled Mr Brown into the cafe, the receptionist hurried off further into the building. Alex hoped it was for some healing supplies. Sure enough, the lady came back with some bandages and first aid material Alex didn't pay heed to. She kneeled down and started tending to Mr Brown's wound. It turned out a large Majenimal – invisible to Alex – had accidently hit Mr Brown hard on the chest. Alex didn't want to see him being treated. He'd already done what he needed to.

He went into a corner of the cafe. The customers had already moved out of the place, aware that there was an emergency. And of course, no one wanted to relax in a Café where a bleeding person lay on the floor at the very entrance.

After questioning the local staff, Alex came to know that there were no hospitals in Sternind, just some basic healing supplies that seemed to cure almost anything other than death.

During the first few minutes in the cafe, Alex was shocked and tensed. But later his tension eased, and he found himself relaxing on a sofa. While Alex was starting to get bored, sitting for almost fifty minutes, Mr Brown appeared in front of him, looking absolutely fine. He flashed his natural smile. 'You're looking as if nothing ever happened.' Alex said.

Mr Brown replied, 'All thanks to Realm Power. So now, shall we get to SIRP? I think your friends might be finishing with their tasks.'

'Yeah, I guess so,' Alex replied.

They both reached SIRP, carefully checking the road for any crazy Majenimals. But actually only Mr Brown could see them as they were invisible to Alex, so basically *he* was careful, while Alex just followed him.

'Should we go in *now*?' Alex asked Mr Brown, hoping the answer to be "Yes".

'Yeah.'

Alex pushed the door open and got into the Institute campus. Though it didn't look like a section of buildings, or floors, but still, he felt something unusual around him. The place was totally white, reaching to the edges of the world seen by him. He was standing on white floor, the walls were white, and the surroundings were the same colour. No object, or anything signifying the existence of a room or building could be seen. Alex didn't know what to think of it all.

'What do you see, Alex?' Mr Brown asked him. Alex told Mr Brown about the whiteness and plainness of the room.

'Well, your imagination is naturally tamed. Now we have to wait for someone to grant us our Access Cards and the permission to perceive the Freshers' room.'

Alex didn't know what all that meant but he got the gist of it. He learned that some "Access Cards" were needed by them to actually be able to see the place and its specific areas. Maybe this condition of their imagination was neutral, and so, everything was appearing white.

Suddenly, Lester came driving out of nowhere in a black Lamborghini which dissolved just as it reached Alex, leaving Lester imbalanced, who fell down. 'Hi, fellas,' he said, standing up.

Angelina arrived from the left side of Alex, shouting "Hiyaaaa" and was apparently ready to impale him in the gut just as her dagger dissolved into thin air. She was dressed in her black suit, but lots of cuts were visible through the places where the fabric had been ripped off. Though Angelina looked like she was in a lot of pain, maybe she had taken over many enemies and emerged as a hero. Her eyes were indicating cruelty, but just as she caught the sight of Alex, Mr Brown, and Lester, something drained from her face, and she transformed into the old sweet Angelina.

'Here he comes,' Mr Brown interrupted before she or Alex had a chance to say something. A humanoid figure emerged from the surroundings. He was an Indian man, wearing a black shirt and white jeans. He looked kind and generous. Alex guessed he was a teacher.

He said in a perfect American accent, 'This sight of Freshers dazzles me. You three are to be given your Access Cards, so follow me. But before that, I'll measure your capability to check if you three are worthy to receive education in Sternind Institute of Realm Power learning or not. Mr Droller Brown, you may go. The principal has orders for you. He is disappointed in you and says that you "did not do as expected, but it worked out fine". You may figure out what the meaning of that message is, while I escort these three to the Freshers' room.'

Mr Brown turned back and left without another word, while the three friends stood staring at the man. 'I must introduce myself. I'm the secretary of order in SIRP. I am also your practical application skills' mentor, Vijay Chakravarti. There were special instructions for me to come and receive you all, though I don't know what the fuss is all about. Now, follow me,' the man said.

Mentor Vijay led them through a series of unapparent turns in the wide white expanse, when he finally and abruptly stopped. He handed them Access Cards, which were red, yellow and violet in colour. Alex received the violet one.

'You three must read out the words embossed on your respective cards in your minds. Do *not* move an inch from where you are standing now, because right now, you three have been engulfed in the mercy symbols of the realms. If you move, you'll burn up. There will be extreme pressure. So try not to let your brain explode, let your fingers leave your hands, or let your soul leave your body. You need to hold everything in place, even the words you'll say in your mind. I repeat, recite them *in your mind*, while keeping your eyes closed. This is just to test your capability and ask the permission to dive into the endless ocean of Realm Power knowledge from the supreme deity of creation, Om,' mentor Vijay said.

Alex did as he had said. The words – "Grant me the

acquiescence to learn RPSBTOUEQELOM" – were really simple, except for the last one. Alex suffered no pain, no problems until he reached the last word. He had trouble pronouncing it, so he settled on speaking it as per the pronunciation of individual letters—Aar-Pee-Es-Bee... But just in the middle of his words, all the things mentor Vijay had said to avoid, started happening. It was really painful. Suddenly, Alex's instincts kicked in. He made up a pronunciation of the last word, saying it as, Rrr-p-s-b-tau-ekelommm. His pain and suffering eased just as he said so. Maybe this was the test of figuring out the things when one was under pressure. He started opening his eyes, just as he heard mentor Vijay's voice, 'Don't open your eyes. You three aren't permitted to be seeing this part of SIRP. I'm not making this up, but still, if you open your eyes now, you all will suffer consequences worse than death. It's just because there are a few security measures in SIRP that have to be followed. I will leave you all here, with the instructions to move straight, and open your eyes just as a warm wind hits you in the face.'

Mentor Vijay's footsteps receded, and Alex did as he was told. He opened his eyes just as a hot wind almost turned his face into Alex kebab. He found himself in a large room, a fireplace burning right next to the entrance. A lot of kids, mostly teens, were hanging out in black suits, just like Alex and his friends. There were lots of accessories in the room, like televisions, video game consoles, weird board games and many bookshelves. 'This might be the Freshers' room,' Alex said.

Angelina agreed sarcastically, 'Yeah. Let's just wait here until further problems come to greet us.'

'Don't think of it like that, Angelina. We can always make new friends. Let's join in the fun,' Lester said.

'You two go on. I need a nap,' Alex said as he retreated on a couch. He soon dozed off into a short nap.

The sleep wasn't peaceful, as he soon woke up due to the loud sounds of the Freshers talking, game consoles beeping, or some mildly loud cheering sounds. He didn't care about anything at that moment. He was just concentrating on the sudden change of events.

All of a sudden, a familiar looking boy sat down next to Alex, muttering, 'What does she think of her...?'

Alex racked his brain, trying to remember who this person was. It clicked him—This guy who had lounged next to him was his classmate from Florida, Kevin. He was Alex's best friend from school. Alex was surprised. Kevin had also been turned to be a teen. Alex was in the company of an old friend!

'My, how did *you* get here?' Alex asked Kevin.

Kevin didn't recognize Alex. 'Do I know you?'

'Of course! Aren't you Kevin Andrew? I'm Alex Drake.'

'Oh, boy. I– I didn't notice you here earlier. It's great to see you!' Kevin said as his face lit up. 'You're a teenager too? I was turned younger during a mission. Guess you've gone through the same. Remember the cannonballs?'

Kevin was naturally hyperactive, and Alex was surprised to be asked questions after a long time. Usually *he* was the one asking questions.

'Uh, no. Actually, my story is a bit different than yours. You were given missions and mysteries, but my case is different.'

'I'll be glad to know. Can't believe you're here! In Sternind!'

Alex told him all he'd gone through after he'd left school. He explained how he received a bit of the business, instead of going to college. He told Kevin in detail about Wasor and his experiences until then, including his suspicions about Vishwaroopaha and Mr Brown. Narrating all that lifted something from his shoulders. It was just like writing in a diary, pouring all his emotions, but the only difference was of written and spoken language.

As Alex finished, Kevin looked awestruck. He said, 'Amazing. I would also like to tell you about my experiences, but… right now, I'm not feeling that good.'

Alex didn't know how to reply to that, but something clicked him. 'Yeah,' he said. 'You were cursing some girl.'

'Exactly! She was *so* boasting about how she did some impossible things—I mean, who can strangle two *anacondas* within a minute? I was fed up of all that nonsense entering my ear. So when I challenged her, she started a goddamn trash talk… And well, I *kinda* lost. I gotta say, she's a devil. A pin-headed stupid devil.'

'Hmm... What's her name?'

'Clairon Johnson. More like Moron Johnson.'

'Uh... O-Okay,' Alex said as he decided to let Kevin

deal with himself. 'I'm gonna just go now. You know, give you time to... Um, gather yourself.'

Kevin didn't reply. Alex got up from the couch, and suddenly a water balloon hit him in the face. He picked up the plastic from his face and threw it on the ground. He looked in the direction from where it had come from, hoping to find the kid who had thrown it. He noticed Angelina, who had made some friends and was unleashing a volley of water balloons on anybody who was within their firing range. As Alex gave her an annoying look, she mouthed the words, **Sorry. Did not mean it.**

Alex scanned the room, and unsurprisingly found that the scene was almost the same as it had been earlier. He found Lester a few metres away, sitting on a wooden chair, his eyes closed. Alex pulled up another one and sat next to him. 'What's up?' he said in a sleepy tone, as he opened his eyes.

'Nothing special. Just met Kevin Andrew there.'

'*What?* You call that *nothing special*?' Lester exclaimed.

'Yup, I met him. In Sternind. In this room. But you must not go to talk to him right now. He said he's not feeling "that good".'

'Me too. I'm just trying to figure out what would be the explanation to the things you asked Mr Brown in the cafe.'

'But, I didn't ask him anything in the cafe. After getting all bloody, he was just being treated in *a cafe*.'

'*What?* This seems intriguing. Tell me in detail.'

And so Alex told Lester about what had happened

when he and Angelina were on their quests to tame their imaginations, including Mr Brown's accident.

Lester's face took up a look of apprehensions. 'That's… terrifying. From now on, I'm not gonna walk on the road.'

'So… You're never even gonna cross the road in Sternind?'

'That,' Lester replied, 'is one thing to think about. Anyway, I think I'm gonna be more careful on the streets now, because, you know, I didn't really feel that good after using the CY devices while walking. I could've fell down.'

'That's a good new year's resolution,' Alex said after he remembered it was the first day of year 2011.

'Cool. You're keeping track of everything,' Lester said as he closed his eyes again.

'No, not really,' Alex replied. 'It just came bobbing in my mind right now. I didn't even think of it earlier. What were you doing while I was napping, by the way?'

Lester didn't say anything, and that's when Alex realized that he'd fallen asleep—*again*.

Alex made up a new year's resolution to keep in touch with his CY device's character Alexander, and to control his clone regularly. He took out his CY device from his pocket and hit the ON button.

Alexander sprang to life on the screen. 'You didn't bring me my CY decoration packs, did you?' he said with a scowl on his face.

Alex smiled. 'I did bring them, Alexander,' he said as

he took out the plastic piece and inserted it into the CY device.

Suddenly, Alexander's outfit changed. He was now looking like a pharaoh from Ancient Egypt. And as suddenly as it happened, the background screen changed. Alexander was standing on an old-fashioned theatre stage, with the curtains drawn out.

'Eww,' Alexander exclaimed as he looked around. 'Doesn't match my clothes.'

He snapped his fingers, and the background changed once again. He was now standing in a desert, with his back facing a large pyramid. 'Now, *that* fits,' he said.

Alex said to him, 'Without any further delay, I want me to get up from bed, brush my teeth, bathe, and do all the regular stuff that one does before breakfast. Then, I need to head for breakfast. I need to not say much, but just comment that the food is tasty. And when I get up from the table, I'll wish everybody a happy new year.'

Alexander tapped his fingers to his head. 'Done, boss.'

'Good. Now get me in my room and enable me to do my… *official business work*, if you know what that is. After Brunch, schedule a meeting with Lester and Angelina's clones. We'll talk and do the same as we do on a regular day.'

'Hmm,' Alexander said. 'You'll have to wait for quite some time, boss. This is gonna take some time. Meanwhile, do you want a view of what your clone is doing? I'll also need you for making a few decisions and handling any surprise events, so don't go anywhere.'

'Yeah, sure. Show me everything. I'm right here.'

The screen changed and Alex saw the world through his clone's eyes. He kept giving orders to Alexander, and Alexander kept calling him "Boss", which lifted his mood. Finally, at the end of the day at Florida, his mother came in his room and asked him what his new year's resolution was. She also mentioned that he hadn't said anything about it the night before, at the party. Alex, quite annoyed, didn't know how the New Year's party had been, as he hadn't been controlling his clone then. Maybe Vishwaroopaha might have taken charge. But anyway, Alex answered his mother's annoying question by saying that his resolution was to help his dad more in business and spend more time with his friends.

At last, he ordered Alexander to make his clone sleep, thus ending the day of controlling his clone in Florida. This all took about an hour. It seemed like a useful device, which helped in utilizing time, rather than wasting it. 'You better more or less repeat what I told you to make my clown do today, `cause I won't be there to give you orders every day,' said Alex to Alexander as he switched off the CY device.

Everything was well managed by then, but still, there were some questions in Alex's mind that Mr Brown hadn't answered. Vishwaroopaha had also promised to meet them at an "Unexpected moment". Alex figured he would ask those questions from Vishwaropaha himself at that very "Unexpected moment".

Suddenly, Mentor Vijay entered the room. He announced, 'Come on, Freshers. The time to judge your experiences, and decide your Grading Groups has come. Form a queue and start following the light in a few minutes.' He snapped his fingers and a blue ball of light appeared hovering in the air.

Alex didn't know what "Grading Groups" were, but he was sure that some process of "judging" *won't* be a pleasant experience.

Chapter 7

Why do concepts have to be so Complicated?

Lester and Angelina were behind him in the queue, but they weren't uttering a single word. Alex wondered what had happened. 'Whatever,' he decided to get his mind off of his friends for a while and focus on what was up next.

Soon, the glowing blue ball of light led the queue to a garden through a series of corridors. It was a magnificent place, perfect for a long picnic. The grass shone brightly in the sunlight. Flowers bloomed here and there, with the sweet company of adorable little creatures—Bees, butterflies and squirrels. The Freshers' exclaims made the place livelier (Though bees weren't what Alex thought of as "ideal" in a beautiful garden, but, he had to go with the saying, "Everything isn't perfect"). At a few instances, squirrels ran past Alex, surprising him just before he smiled.

Alex couldn't help but think about how he was going to be… Judged? Now? He was not sure. How would *he* be judged? There usually is a case in a judicial court which is judged by the so-called judges, or there's some kind of performance in a contest which is "judged". But how can a person judge another person without acknowledging that their judgement is based on their perspective of that person—Good, Bad, Arrogant, Kind, Punctual? Precisely, how can a man judge another man by not adjusting his views of the other man's qualities as per his judgement?

This doubt of Alex was cleared when Mentor Vijay, who was already in the garden, raised himself up in the air using Realm Power, and said to everyone, 'Now, to quickly get judged into four Grading Groups, you all need to assemble in pairs. Remember, this is no subgroup, rather temporary measures necessary for judging and assigning you into the four groups.' He suddenly stopped, looking confused. He grumbled, 'I *know* should've made them single seater, but no. The principal insisted. How can it be a "Bonding" experience…?' He then returned to his serious glare and continued, 'Remember to pair with your friend whom you've known the longest. You have to be with the Sternindian whom you've known from Earth, or if you don't have a friend from Earth amidst us here, then it must be the one whom you have met here in Sternind recently. Now quickly, divide yourselves into groups of two and come to me pair by pair. This is a test of your qualities. Precisely, your determination, time management, hard work, and fate. There are four

Grading Groups that determine the related quality you possess. They are – you guessed it – Time, Hard Work, Fate, and Determination.'

Everyone was now divided into groups of two. Alex was with Lester, and Angelina was with... was that Clairon? Kevin was with some blonde girl. Alex guessed that she could be Kevin's sister her brother liked making fun of, Marrisa Andrew. She was a beautiful girl, with sharp eyes, fair skin, long hair, long legs and a sweet voice.

'Wait, Mr Chakravarti. Today, I myself will be judging the Freshers,' said a heavy and familiar voice from behind. Alex and Lester turned back.

And there he was. Indeed, it was "a very unexpected moment". Vishwaroopaha, dressed in a superman costume, shot a quick glance at everyone said confidently, 'I'll do it all quickly. After all, I need to tell them the basics, and today we're not going to have an assembly.' He pointed at himself. 'Because we have a fancy dress day today, don't you remember?'

'Oh, yeah. Sure I do, respected principal,' Mr Chakravarti said with a sigh as he trudged off back into the building, probably wondering how childish an idea like "Fancy Dress Day" was in such an Institute.

Alex's jaw dropped. Vishwaroopaha—The principal of SIRP? How could it be? How could he become the principal of SIRP from a simple magical helper in less than a year? There was something fishy. 'Either he's not Vishwaroopha, or was Wasor Island…? That symbol...' Alex was confused.

Vishwaroopaha cleared his throat. 'We shall not stall here now, shall we?' he said, smiling. 'Before dividing– or should I say uniting…? Because when you all get divided into Grading Groups, you indeed are united as students of SIRP. So, before *uniting* you all, I want to clear some things that most of the Freshers question when they read the book about the concepts of Realms. They question a lot when they get through the tests, and when they get their Supporters. Speaking of Supporters… I think you all haven't received your Majenimals, have you?'

'No,' the group of Freshers said in unison.

'Very well. You'll receive them after clearing the SCT—Support Cooperation Test. It is an examination conducted once a year in SIRP. So for now, there's no need to worry about Majenimals. You'll be notified later. There's a lot to explain, but I'll do my best.' He spread the fingers of his right hand, joined their tips together to make a vague cone, and then separated them again. He did some particular movements with his fingers in the air, and suddenly, a stage appeared in the garden. Successively, as Vishwaroopaha went up the steps, plastic chairs appeared next to each Fresher. Alex quickly grabbed one and seated himself. Lester sat down adjacent to him.

'Okay, let's do this formally. Greetings, Freshers. I am SIRP's principal since four hundred and seventy-eight years. Yes, that's true. The average age of a person in Sternind is two thousand five hundred years. That's because the air and environment of Sternind is purer than that of Earth, since Sternind has no cars, factories or whatever fancy polluting devices they use in Earth. Anyway, my name is Alfred Crest, though I prefer the name Vishwaroopaha,' Vishwaroopaha said as he looked at Alex for a second and winked.

Alex was shocked. Vishwaroopaha truly *was* very old, but not two thousand years old, obviously. The reason Alex found this man unbelievable and a little untrustworthy earlier was mostly because he was a liar. Why had he lied... What had he done... How had he done it... Alex had no idea about what were Vishwaroopaha's plans for him. He also had no idea what he was thinking about at that very moment. He decided to receive the answers to his innumerable questions anyhow and as soon as possible.

Vishwaroopaha continued his speech, 'As you all know, we are here to clarify the terms of your education and boarding in SIRP. Those of you whose parents are Sternindians must form a separate group and haul your chairs to form a cluster aside from the other faction. Be quick.'

The children did as he instructed. 'Very well,' he said. 'I know what you all feel like. There are a lot of questions burning into your curious minds. Though I have another book that I could hand you all, and be done with this speech, but I'm actually one of those who pay heed to each and every detail of all the events in SIRP.' He stopped for a moment, giving the audience a look like **You understand you can't escape me, don't you?** He continued a moment later, 'So, to save you all from the trouble of reading another fat book, we must begin!'

There was some murmuring among the crowd.

'There's a long list of questions I encounter every year, but I'll only clarify the basic stuff,' he continued after a pause. 'First of all, I must talk about the Access Cards you have been given. To keep away any kind of evil power, spirit or Majenimal, SIRP has a complete illusion and multi-dimensional safety system. You all saw some rooms and corridors on the way to this assembly point, and that was only after you got admission in SIRP. Believe me, you didn't see the institute's actual rooms there. Those were just illusions. Before admission in SIRP, anyone entering into the building, can only see an endless expanse of white surroundings. After admission, one can see only the Freshers' rooms and the illusions. After being granted Access Cards and getting divided into Grading Groups, one can see SIRP in its true form. But, if I say that SIRP has no true form, how would you react? Confused, right? I'll get to that in a bit. Now, I want to ask, are there any queries?'

Alex wished he could ask "Alfred" about the trick he had been playing on him and his friends since he had met him at Wasor. He wanted to ask that in a really angry tone, but in private.

Nobody said anything, which showed that no more clarification was required on the topic Vishwaroopaha/Alfred had talked about until then.

'Right,' Alfred continued. 'No questions. So, I *am* now saying that there is no true form of SIRP. This is a security measure, to keep out the ones who aren't admitted in the institute, but it serves another purpose too. As you all know, imagination is the key. You all have tamed your imagination, but still, a lot more is to go in the process of learning Realm Power. So, the teachers have created their own classrooms by imagination which can be anywhere in the campus, and you all have to locate them via your Access Cards, AOPs and above all, imagination. Now you might be thinking why to have so many confusing concepts when we could have had a predefined structure and avoided the fuss. My answer is that, it all has a plus point. Sometimes, people want to be alone, not even in the company of friends. Though none of you would admit it in the presence of your buddies, but at your age, it happens. You all change from kids into teens and then adults. There is a transformation. Some of you may feel extra annoyed, or a little less happy, or depressed. But that's not the main point. Sometimes, you need to be with your friends, and away from your enemies. Though I request all of you to not pick a fight – verbal or physical – with any of the students, still, it isn't possible that all of you can become friends like a big joint family. You will have rows for sure. So, the plus point I mentioned earlier is that in order to have privacy, or some defence from foes, *you* all can create your own rooms as per your desires in SIRP anytime in between classes, or after school. The Access Cards sense the presence of an imaginative room, and can be used to seek permission to enter in a room, or classrooms. Though there are already such rooms for boys' and girls' dorms, the classes and the "practical application skills" class grounds, any student or teacher can create any private imaginative room. But remember, the teachers have supremacy over each private room, which means that they can enter in the room anytime without having to ask for permission. There is a short booklet on how to use Access Cards to enter in or create an imaginative room and what and when all lessons are there in the first year of education in SIRP. You will be provided that. Any queries?'

Again, Alex was stunned by Vishwaroopaha's words. Many things made sense now—The weirdness of Sternind, and the concepts of SIRP—Many of them. Alex had no questions at all this time. So did the children around him. Nobody said anything. Even Lester looked entranced.

'At the moment, I must explain why I separated you Freshers into groups based on your parentage. It's not discrimination, rather, I need to know how many of you will be staying in the dorms and how many of you will just attend regular school, ending at five o'clock. The Mentors need the list to make your beds ready and prevent any sharp-toothed critter from eating your body parts or making chaos in your bed sheet. They'll soon receive the list concerning it all, I think.' He smiled and looked at a boy among the crowd, who was about seventeen years old. He had keen eyes and an intelligent expression. He mouthed, **Me?** The face looked familiar to Alex, but he couldn't remember who the boy was. His concentration on finding the boy's name was broken by Vishwaroopaha, who continued, 'By the way, the booklet will be provided to you all. For now, if any of you wish, you can take part in today's Fancy Dress Day. And it's quite late, so I won't think of conducting the Grading Groups' division proceedings now. Farewell, until we meet again tomorrow in the morning assembly hall. We'll get you all into your Grading Groups then and there. Meanwhile, I'll get to my office and grant your Access Cards the temporary permission to perceive SIRP,' Vishwaroopaha finished as he went down the stage stairs and headed towards the building.

'Now is the time,' Alex thought. He grabbed Lester by his wrist and ran towards Alfred (Or Vishwaroopaha. Or Mr V. Alex was getting crazy by only thinking of those names) . He stopped in front of him, blocking his path. 'Oh, look who it is! Nice to meet you, student. Now, kindly make way for me...' Vishwaroopaha said.

'Really?' Alex said as he brought out his AOP and pointed it at Vishwaroopaha's chest. Vishwaroopaha's eyes widened on the sight of the Primo. Alex dug the Primo's wooden fingers a little deeper into Vishwaroopaha's chest. 'Oh no, you don't,' he said.

Vishwaroopaha again flashed a smile on his face. 'Adorable, Alex. Your way of dealing with unexpected situations is really adorable. You are a star, boy. You proved your braveness yet again,' he said.

Alex was amazed. He had thought that Vishwaroopaha had forgotten him after he landed them into Sternind and turned them into children. Alex had thought that that was how Vishwaroopaha would bring some selected Freshers in SIRP. First he would endanger their lives, then save them, gaining their trust, and then send them here by giving them a book which would instruct them to go to a place where they would face their death. But it was not so. A mere test. This incident brought the fact to Alex's attention that Vishwaroopaha indeed had a way with words.

'We'll talk,' the so-called Alfred said as he did the same movement with his fingers which he had done on the stage. Alex braced himself for the appearance of plastic chairs. Instead, comfy recliners solidified next to each of them. Alex was amazed yet again. 'I see the look of awe on your face. The thing is, the less big the operation, the better the quality,' Alfred said as he gestured towards the recliners.

'See, I'm sorry. I'm sorry for all that happened to you three. I found some potential in you, Alex, and I selected you to become a Sternindian. I figured you would need special attention and advanced tasks to be prepared for Sternind. You and your friends have passed the test,' Alfred continued.

'What do you mean by "advanced tasks"?' Lester asked.

'Of course, the challenges at Wasor. Didn't you know the challenges were fake, made by Mr Brown? The cops… Why do you think they seemed possessed at that time when they told your parents about Wasor? They were all under control of Mr Brown. Surely he must have divulged this information, didn't he?'

'He didn't. Because he knew he was going to be smashed badly into Brown pulp if he told us,' Alex said in an angry tone. 'I suspected this way earlier, but was just waiting for conformation. Guess we have it now. Anyway, I need to inform Angelina about this,' Alex thought, but maybe Lester was having the same thought, as he said, 'I'll just fill Angelina in on this… stuff. Will be back with her in a minute,' and went away.

'Let's not dwell on the past, right?' Alfred asked Alex when Lester moved out of earshot. 'Anyway, that's what the saying is, I think,' he muttered a few seconds later, when he received no reply from Alex.

'What was the reason behind all that Mr Brown did to us? Tell me clearly. I just don't want the answer to be *fate*, which you and Mr Brown have been constantly holding responsible every time you give an answer.'

'Oh, it's simple. They were all tests and coincidences. The liquefaction… That was your mistake, Alex. Or Droller's lack of speaking the crux on time. That little trip to space… You know why that had to be done. Your wish, and a little test of you and your friends' Supporters.'

Alex gave Vishwaroopaha – Alex had finally got over his dilemma and decided to call him that – an uneasy look, still not knowing the answers to many other things.

'I know that expression on the Freshers' faces,' Vishwaroopaha said. 'Ask me the thing that has been troubling you the most, Alex.'

'All this time, I had been trying to understand how life was in Sternind, hoping to get the answer to this main query. Even when I got the clarification of almost all the questions, this one still kept bothering me. I want to ask that why are these… These *Freshers* here? Why are *we* here? What is the main motive of *living* in Sternind? Getting educated about Realm Power? If you don't have answers to any of those, why did your ancestors even *find* Sternind?'

Vishwaroopaha chuckled. 'I just love it when curious minds shower me with questions. Alex, this all is to make Sternind as good as, or even better than Earth. I know you don't know what this means, but I can make you understand in a simpler way. Imagine Earth is a person, with good manners, good lifestyle but with mediocre talent. Imagine Sternind as another person, with mediocre manners, not-so-good lifestyle but amazing talent. People can cope up with the one who has less talent but is disciplined, but it's not the same with the one who is mannerless but amazing in his/her abilities. By manners, in our case, I mean, the landscape of a Realm. Earth is naturally beautiful, with spellbinding sceneries. But Sternind… Well, you know how this Realm looks like since you have been in the observatory. In my example, by lifestyle, I mean, social evils. Earth is developed, with some unity among nations. Even though there're separate cultures and nations in that Realm, it manages to avoid many so-called "World Wars". But Sternind… There are many political leaders and provinces, with large armies, and there's a lot of racial discrimination throughout the Realm. Even though Sternind is one body, one country, with just state divisions called "Prants", these problems are turning Sternind into a battlefield, where there are fights for supremacy, leading to mass destruction. The "Talent" of the two "people" Earth and Sternind I mentioned, is the talent in technology, or supernatural qualities. Precisely, talent is the thing that can help a Realm accomplish anything. So, the main motive of SIRP is to educate people to stay united in our Prant of Sternind. We do this in the hope that someday… someday… Sternind would be better than Earth in… overall qualities.'

Alex got his answer, but there was still one thing he wasn't able to believe. Sure, the deadly challenges could be fake, but Cloedboriogd's story... That *had* to be fake too. Maybe Angelina was playing a prank on him... But that couldn't be true, because when Alex had met her during the ninth challenge, she was actually very cold, just like her description of her experiences with Cloedboriogd. It all contradicted...

Alex decided to ask Vishwaroopaha about what it was, then and there. But he didn't get the chance. 'Well, I guess I'm done here for the day. If you need me, Alex, concentrate on your imagination. I'll surely answer. Do remember, imagination is the one and only flawless and fool-proof way of communication in Sternind. There is absolutely no need to construct large mobile phone signal towers... Ugh, those people… But anyway, bye for now. Hope to see you tomorrow!' Vishwaroopaha ended as he snapped his fingers in yet another weird way and disappeared in a yellow cloud of smoke, taking his recliner with him.

Alex got up from his comfy chair and hurried towards his friends. They were just getting up to leave the cluster of plastic chairs, when Alex said, 'No need to come. Vishwaroopaha's already done his *disappearing-into-smoke* thing.'

Alex was feeling nauseous. He didn't know why, but the feeling automatically settled inside him as if to say, **Let's see what you can do to get me off. Betcha aren't even brave and strong enough to shake me off, much less suspect that the island had been fake and you had been at lack of knowing the truth all the time.**

Alex felt bad. He made an excuse, 'I think I'm gonna puke. Excuse me,' and walked away to sit on a chair far from them. He *really* needed some personal space at that time.

Alex didn't realize how he had fallen asleep in such a condition. He was woken up by Lester, who was trying to get his attention by hitting him on the shoulder, 'Bro, it's quite dark now. Let's get going to the dormitory'.

'Yeah, right,' replied Alex as he got up. The weather suddenly turned cold. It was night time, and the sky was devoid of clouds. No one except a few kids other than Alex and Lester were still in the garden.

As they headed back towards the building, a question popped up in Alex's mind. He asked Lester, 'Hey, didn't you take part in the Fancy Dress Day? Your clothes are… Nothing special. Just the same suit…'

'Yeah. Didn't feel like it. But Angelina did. She dressed up as a black cat. It was kind of funny, when I looked at her face. The whiskers made her look totally stupid. She was having fun, though. With her new best buddy Clairon…'

'Hmm… Do you remember that Angelina had paired up with Clairon Johnson, the girl whom she had met in Sternind? By the rules, she had to pair up with one of us, as we are Sternindians now and we know her from earlier than Clairon does. We know her from when she was a little kid. Then… why did she stand with Clairon?'

Lester shrugged and replied, 'There's three of us. At least one had to be left out if we made pairs of two. Angelina was left idle. But dunno why she was with Clairon. Maybe… Clairon really *was* Angelina's friend from Earth, maybe they became friends at the same time we became Angelina's friends, or they were pals even *before* that… Can't make sense of it.'

'I think, what you said can be possible, the same way Kevin and I are buddies. Likewise, Angelina and Clairon might be.'

Lester said, 'You never know what's up with girls.'

'You're right, man,' Alex replied as he fist-bumped Lester.

They soon reached the boys dorm, locating their way via some signs put up especially for the Freshers. It was just a normal place, with no special arrangements or anything unusual. Alex located his bunk bed and climbed on it. 'Have those booklets arrived?' he asked Lester, who was sitting on his bed, not far from Alex.

'Yup. They're in that cupboard. I'm not really anxious to read them tonight, though. Have had enough for a day…'

'Me too. We'll just figure it all out tomorrow. But… I don't know when the classes are starting. We must check out the timetable… Hey, Lester, should I get you a copy, too?'

'Nah. You go through the schedule, and wake me up an hour before the assembly,' Lester said as he lay down on his bed.

Alex went over to the cupboard Lester had pointed towards. He opened it and brought out the booklet. It was titled, SCHEDULE FOR FRESHERS IN SIRP. 'Typical,' Alex thought as he climbed back onto his bunk, with the booklet in hand. He started reading. There was nothing special in it; just basic and easy techniques for using the Access Cards and the class schedule for each Grading Group. But then Alex remembered that they hadn't been divided into Grading Groups, so the schedule was of no use for now. Maybe Lester had forgotten it too, or he was simply too tired to think about it.

The only useful information he received was how to make use of the Access Cards and the timing of the morning assembly. He kept it all in mind and put the booklet aside.

'Goodnight, Lester,' he said as he rested his head against the soft pillow. He heard Lester's voice in reply, 'See ya tomorrow!'

Alex said, 'You know we're just a few metres away, right?'

'Yeah, but still, I *will* see you tomorrow, right?' Lester said.

'That wasn't an appropriate greeting for the moment, but yeah, now that you've explained, it makes sense,' Alex replied sarcastically

'Mhm. Now go to bed.'

'Alright, man. Guess I'll see you tomorrow.'

Alex didn't know it yet, but this would be the first and last peaceful sleep he'd get at SIRP.

He climbed out of his bunk in the morning, rubbing his eyes. Not many boys were up. Some were writing in their notebooks, sitting on their bunks. 'Diaries,' Alex thought. Whereas, some of them were heading out of the dormitory. 'On their way to the morning assembly hall, I think,' Alex thought.

He looked around. Lester was still asleep. As Alex woke him up, he muttered, 'No, mom. I'm not gonna go to school today…' Alex hit him hard on his arm, and suddenly his eyes fluttered open. He glanced at Alex, who was sitting at his bedside, and said, 'That hurt.'

'There was no other way. Now get up, man,' Alex said.

He helped Lester sit up. Alex freshened up in the bathroom. Lester was next. They soon got ready for the morning assembly.

'So,' Lester asked when they had sauntered back to Lester's bed. 'Will there be another queue? Or… Do we have to get to the place by ourselves?'

'We're on our own, I guess. Let's find the assembly hall by the so-called "imagination".'

Both of them headed out of the boys dorm. The place had changed. Instead of the corridors they had seen the day before, Alex saw just fog and mist all around them; he could only make out a hazy bit of some pillars with inscriptions and miniature statues of deities carved on them. Unfortunately, it brought back bad memories.

'Am I seeing things,' Lester asked, clutching Alex's arm. 'Or has this portion of the building actually changed?'

'Changed in what sense? Tell me clearly. I see foggy surroundings. What are you looking at?'

'Same.'

'Okay, then. It *has* changed.' Alex told Lester. 'I think we have to use some kind of a tracking technique in our minds to find the assembly hall. Concentrate on imagination, hmm… Let's do it.'

'Yeah.'

Alex closed his eyes and started scanning the building, using the same 3-D grid. He found out that it was made like a tall skyscraper, having about two hundred floors. He also noticed various classrooms and dining rooms, along with an elevator. But he was mainly focusing on finding the assembly hall. To his surprise, it was on the top floor.

He opened his eyes at almost the same moment Lester did. He said, 'I've found the hall. Follow me.'

'Nah. *You* follow me,' Lester replied as he closed

his eyes and started running at a fast speed towards a particular direction. Alex bounded after him.

He shouted, 'Where are you taking us? The hall is on the top floor!'

He received Lester's reply, 'Run without asking any questions. All I can say is we are going close to the girls' dorm.'

'You were looking at *girls*? Dude, that's kinda... inappropriate, you know. We were only supposed to locate the assembly hall!'

'No questions!'

Alex grumbled in disapproval but did as he was asked to. He couldn't lose track of his friend in this "imaginative" and misty hell of a building as he ran after him. He soon stopped, as Lester came to a halt at a particular spot. The scene was shocking. A few girls were giggling and laughing as they pointed towards another girl who was breathing heavily, as she lay on the floor.

"Lay" wasn't the appropriate word for her. She looked as if she was beaten badly, and pushed with enough force to knock her down onto the floor. Her hair was a mess. Her cheeks were almost as red as a cherry. She had an expression of hate and contempt on her face.

The girl was Angelina Barrette.

Alex helped her get up. 'What happened? Why did they do this to you?' he asked the twelve-year-old, in a tone that could've made anybody believe that Alex was her protective big brother.

Lester forged ahead towards the group of girls, an

I'll kill you look on his face. The girls bolted at once.

Meanwhile, Alex got his answer from Angelina. 'Humiliation. Fight. Ka-Blam,' she said, which explained the situation.

'Who were those no-good losers?' Lester asked Angelina, turning back.

'They say someone named Alicia gave them orders. Alicia received orders from Willie. Willie received orders from Neha. Neha was given instructions by… Ugh. Forget it. All I can say is that those girls weren't doing it on purpose. At instances I could see incoherent expressions on their faces. It seemed like… They were being *possessed*,' Angelina replied.

'We'll soon get to the root of the matter. It might be indirect ragging done by someone, using Realm Power,' Alex said.

'Yeah… It must be so,' said Angelina, who started tidying up her hair, straightening her clothes and her expression.

'Lester, how did you know that this was happening?' Alex asked, intrigued.

'I guess I can locate emergencies using Realm Power. I don't know how, it just kinda happens,' Lester said. 'And also, we must get to the assembly hall now. Alex, take the lead,' Lester said.

'Great,' Alex muttered. '*Now* you're asking me to take the lead.'

They followed him to the nearest elevator, which was made up of gold, or was it golden colour? The symbol of

SIRP was etched on its two rectangular parting doors. There was no elevator music playing inside, and Alex soon got to know the reason when he pressed the "FLOOR 203" button, which would lead them to the assembly hall. They reached the floor in not more than five seconds. The whooshing sound of the elevator made up for it.

The view was so exhilarating that Alex almost jumped off the building. The place was not like an assembly hall at all. It was an open area, with a large balcony overlooking a magnificent landscape of Sternind. There were chairs arranged in a systematic order, and an elegant stage was constructed in front of them. There were stalls at regular intervals, offering many kinds of foods and games.

Children and teachers milled around here and there, talking, eating or just roaming aimlessly to admire Floor 203.

'This,' Angelina said, 'is–'

She was cut off by Vishwaroopaha. 'Ahem,' he said, as he appeared out of thin air abruptly, wearing white robes. 'I see that you three have navigated your way here. Well, then. Welcome. Welcome to Floor 203. Before I start the process of assigning Grading Groups to Freshers, I'd like to ask something. Have any of you noticed anything peculiar? I mean, out of the blue. Of course, everything may seem strange to you in the first few days of being in Sternind, but my question remains. Report anything to me that's… Distracting you three.'

Alex was suspicious. He asked Vishwaroopaha, 'Why are you asking this to us?'

Vishwaroopaha smiled. 'Your Supporter caught my

eye.' His expression turned guarded abruptly. 'It's, uhh… Something special.'

'No,' Angelina said quickly. 'I think we're good. We haven't witnessed anything unusual at all, thank you very much.'

'Alright, then. I'll conduct the assembly shortly. Meanwhile, help yourselves to some breakfast,' said Vishwaroopaha as he marched away.

'Why didn't you tell him?' Lester asked Angelina.

'I felt it was not right to tell him right now. And I really don't want any more quests or challenges for us to complete. It would just mean more suffering. I'm better off with being under control of Cloedboriogd,' she replied, with a dangerous look in her eyes.

'I'm sorry to say,' Alex interrupted, 'but I must mention that you are a walking time bomb. You can be possessed by Cloedboriogd anytime. You are going to turn evil, sooner or later. We have to be ready for any kind of suffering if that means Vishwaroopaha would tell us a way to get that demon's influence off of you.'

'This is enough talk,' Angelina said in an angry tone, 'You must keep in mind that we're here to learn, and enjoy. So don't ruin that. We don't even know what lies ahead of us in Sternind and you're going on and on with my probability of turning evil.' She didn't wait for Alex's reply but headed towards a food stall titled SOOTHING ICE CREAM.

'Wouldn't like it if I would have ice cream as the first meal in breakfast,' Lester commented, no doubt trying to calm down Alex. Truly, Alex was shocked by this behaviour of Angelina. What was happening to her?

'Is it Cloedboriogd?' he asked Lester, not knowing what he was thinking.

'Where?' Lester looked around.

'No, I'm not saying he's here. I mean that, is he the one responsible for Angelina being like... *this*?'

'Chill, bro. She might be just a bit cranky because of her experience with those girls.'

But Alex couldn't believe it. Angelina's attitude... Vishwaroopaha's question and his sudden interest in Alex's Supporter... It seemed connected. Alex stood there for a while, thinking.

Finally, Lester spoke up. 'I'm gonna go have some food. Follow me, will you?'

'Um... Okay,' Alex said.

After they had had a pretty decent breakfast, they got themselves seated in the second row of chairs facing the main stage.

Suddenly, he noticed a boy spilling a drink on his white shirt. Curious, Alex then scanned the surroundings. Many of the students were wearing black suits, and many had coloured velvets on, but most of them were dressed casually.

Alex bumped Lester on his elbow and asked, 'Hey, is there any dress code for students here?'

'Nope. "Freedom" is emphasised in SIRP, just like back home in America. And those guys like us in the black suits? That's the complimentary dress for Freshers.

And those people in the coloured clothing, that's the dress of your Grading Group allotted to you after you get judged. That's complimentary, too. It's all up to you whether you wanna wear that or not. All I know is that they spend a lot on the students.'

'Wow. How do *you* know all this? Studied some books all night?'

Lester smiled. 'Learned many things yesterday while you were asleep on that plastic chair.'

'Ah.'

Orchestral music blared suddenly from some invisible speakers, which reminded Alex of the grand introduction of a famous movie production company. Vishwaroopaha climbed on the stage. He started with greetings, and said many things about various subjects Alex couldn't understand. Finally, he came over to the subject of dividing the Freshers into Grading Groups.

'And now, Freshers, please form pairs. Remember, this is no subgroup. You all just need to form pairs according to the rules Mr Chakravarti gave yesterday, which is only for the classification ceremony. After that, you all are free to be with anybody you want during the time between classes, regardless of their Grading Group. Your Grading Group is only the batch of students you will be taking classes with,' said Vishwaroopaha.

The Freshers assembled in pairs. Most of the people had chosen the same partners they had paired up with the day before. Naturally, Alex was with Lester and Angelina with Clairon.

Many pairs approached Vishwaroopaha one by one, and when he would do a single twirling of his index finger, the two kids would disappear into thin air. This process continued until only a handful of Freshers were left. Soon, Angelina and Clairon headed up to Vishwaroopaha. He said a few words to them and then sent them on their way, by dispersing their bodies into air.

Next came Alex and Lester's turn. As they reached Vishwaroopaha, he said, smiling, 'All you need to do now is stay vigilant and fear nothing. You'll feel as if you're going to be dead, and if you overcome your apprehensions in the process—*poof*! You have your Grading Group! Now, get ready. It's going to be a rough ride.'

Alex noticed that Vishwaroopaha had carefully chosen his words. He had framed them so that nobody would have more than a vague idea of what would happen in the classification ceremony. Vishwaroopaha hadn't said *going to be smacked dead* or *going to be shot dead* or just dying *out of fear*. He had kept all of it anonymous. Alex wondered what kind of a terrific – or terrifying – experience this would be.

As soon as Vishwaroopaha twisted his index finger again, Alex found himself in a cart moving on a track along with Lester. This reminded Alex of some sort of a game he had played, in which the cart would roll on endlessly on the tracks. The surroundings were pretty dark. There was nothing much around the tracks except deep pits on either side, some creepy looking Annabelle-like dolls and some Halloween pumpkins on a few raised platforms. Alex was used to darkness, given his experiences with *DarkService* and the cave where Lester had been imprisoned at Wasor. He wasn't fazed by such a change in the surroundings. However, Lester looked like he was going to wet his pants.

'It's all right, dude,' Alex assured him, 'It's just, um... A test. Stay sane. We're just getting throu–*ooo*' he was interrupted just as the cart abruptly increased its speed to about seventy miles per hour. The wind smacked Alex in the air a thousand times before he made sense of what was happening. He ducked down to avoid the high air drag with his eyes just peeping over the cart's boundary walls.

Lester, however, was late to realize the change, and was blown out of the cart. Suddenly, as Alex looked back, the solid ground behind him turned into a black bottomless pit and swallowed Lester. 'Lester!' Alex shouted, but he knew that it was of no use. Lester was "judged", not dead. At least that was what Alex thought of the incident in order to assure himself that everything was alright.

He then looked up front. A large black screen appeared for just a moment with the word HARD WORK displayed on it. Alex understood that Lester was classified into that group, leaving him to find a place in some The screen dissipated into air just as quickly as it had appeared leaving behind some colourful wisps of smoke.

Alex stayed vigilant. He noticed a sharp blade jutting out of a dark spot at neck-level with him. Had he been a split second late in inclining his head sideways, he could have been decapitated.

He then kept his eyes trained on every suspicious thing he spotted until it was out of sight. He could *not* afford to be blown away into oblivion, or get into a Grading Group as a severed head. The ride soon became tougher. Ghouls and skeletons would pop out of nowhere, causing Alex to scream. He started spotting more sharp objects than earlier. The number and size of the scary dolls increased.

Soon, a moment arrived when large trolls wearing nothing but a loincloth appeared out of nowhere and began stomping objects all around them. Alex figured he had very less time to think of something before the giants turned him into red-sauce—*red-blood* pasta. He strained his head and eyes, trying to find some loophole or gather some useful information, but all he could manage was not dying of fear. To his surprise, the trolls did not step on him, rather destroyed everything. Alex seriously loved the sight of a menacing Annabelle being crushed by the foot of a smelly troll.

More cart tracks appeared around Alex, and the strength of the trolls increased.

He felt a sudden blow towards the left side of the cart, and barely saved himself from falling down as the cart was derailed. He climbed out of it and started dodging the trolls' feet, managing to get past them. What he didn't know was that the trolls were after him, but they were just not killing him. When Alex wasn't looking back, one of them hit him with his large leg, sending him tumbling. He hit his head very badly on a hard surface, but didn't lose blood. He was alright, though the pain was intense. What had happened with Lester, also happened with him. The ground turned into a black pit, and he fell, screaming.

He fell down, only to find himself standing again in the Assembly hall, but wearing different clothes. He now had a stylish blue and black shirt and trousers on. On the sleeves were some letters stitched in an elegant writing with golden colour—*Determination*.

He smiled. At last, he was "judged". He figured – or at least hoped – that most of the hardships to accustom him and his friends into the local society of this Prant of Sternind were over. Thinking about Prants, Alex remembered that he had forgotten to ask Mr Brown what this Prant was called. He made a mental note to ask someone about it. But right then, he had to find his friends and get to know about their Grading Groups. Though Lester wasn't with him, Alex hoped that at least Kevin or Angelina might be there in the same Grading Group as Alex.

He started looking through the crowd, and soon spotted Lester and Angelina. They were talking to each other, their dresses also changed. Angelina was rocking a red and black outfit, while Lester had a dark green shirt with dark blue pants on. This clarified that the three of them were assigned to different Grading Groups. The "judging" didn't go as Alex had hoped, but still, being classified in different Grading Groups wasn't going to faze their friendship. That was what he expected the situation to be like from then on.

Shaking these thoughts aside, he approached his friends. 'Wassup?' he said, as he couldn't think of another way to start a conversation.

'Hey, Alex,' said Angelina.

'So,' Lester asked, turning towards Alex. 'Your Grading Group?'

'Determination.'

'*What?*'

'What's so shocking in that? I see many people around here wearing the same clothes as me.'

'It's nothing, Alex,' said Angelina, 'It's just that… I– *We* have figured that Freshers don't usually get into the Determination Grading Group. You can only hope to get assigned to that group in your third or fourth year. *You* getting into that Grading Group… This just means… More obstacles, more bad luck…'

Alex raised an eyebrow. 'And from where did you both get to know this nonsense?' he inquired.

'Well, we sort of found that out in the Grading Group post-judging instruction manual,' said Lester.

'Wha– Dude, is that even a thing? Who *lets* these guys publish such baloney? And well, even if it *is* a thing, we'll see to it later. Let's just… You know what, drop that matter for now. What *I* wanna know is *your* Grading Group, Angelina.'

Before Angelina could reply, Lester whined, 'Don't you care about *me*?'

'I know you've been assigned to Hard Work, Lester.

A screen appeared in front of me for a brief time after you fell from the cart. It displayed your GG's name,' replied Alex.

Angelina said, 'GG, huh? Nice short form, I think. We'll use that from now on. And oh, I'm in the GG Time.'

'Hmm… Dunno what this has to do with our lives. These GGs' names are virtues; they do seem to relate to something. My GG's name relates to me, I think. Yours, too, Lester. But… Dunno what Time has to do with Angelina. I'm still thinking that why didn't any of us get sorted into Fate…'

'You know what, buddy,' Lester said, with an unusual look on his face, 'I think the answer to all these questions is the fourth Grading Group itself. It's just… Fate. Let life go on, man. Just see what happens. That's who a free-minded and jolly person is. I think you'll soon learn the answers to these questions, and the one who's gonna teach you isn't going to be any person—Not Vishwaroopaha, not Mr Brown. You'll only learn from life and experiences from now on.'

To Alex's astonishment, Lester suddenly morphed into Vishwaroopaha. The principal of SIRP stood before them now, smiling as usual. 'Greetings, Alex and Angelina. I just changed shape into your friend Lester for a few minutes now to check on you without being recognized. You know, I have noticed that you both seem uneasy whenever I'm around. So I just tried taking Lester's form. I hope I didn't offend you, did I?'

'No, not at all,' said Angelina through gritted teeth.

'Good, then,' Vishwaroopaha replied, ignoring the expression.

Anger bubbled inside Alex. What did Vishwaroopaha think of himself? He was just about to shout curses but stopped himself when Vishwaroopaha said, 'By the way,' Vishwaroopaha said just before he vanished in air, 'you two must go meet your real friend now. He's stuffing his mouth with a burger at a food stall. Good day, until we meet again!'

After reuniting with Lester, Alex told him about what had happened. Lester seemed shocked, but didn't say much. Maybe he was getting used to such surprises. Anyway, the three of them decided to bid goodbye and meet at dusk, after classes.

Alex headed back to the Boys' dorm, checked the timetable, and successively kept it in his pocket. The Freshers of all the four Grading Groups had a common first period—Class of Introduction, by Mentor Michael Bolt.

Alex made his way to the classroom using his imagination. Just where the invisible classroom's invisible door was located, he used his Access Card just as it had been described in the booklet. He swiped the edges of the card in some invisible sockets to form certain patterns, as described in the booklet. At last, for his own unique identity, he had to sign on an invisible board using the edges of his access card.

The entrance became visible, and Alex could see a solid wooden door in front of him. He pushed it open, revealing a large classroom filled with desks and chairs, most of them occupied. Their teacher Michael Bolt was not in the room, though Alex suspected he would be there any moment. He quickly located and took a seat while searching for Lester. Alex noticed Lester was talking to some kids he didn't know, maybe he was trying to make new friends. He decided to leave him alone for some time and started looking around for Kevin. He spotted him a few feet away, sitting alone. Before he could consider approaching him, Mentor Bolt appeared. Proclaiming his arrival, red light filled the room. Then it narrowed down to several moving rods of laser, and collected together in the center of the room to form the silhouette of a man, which then solidified into Mentor Michael Bolt. He stood before the baffled Freshers, smiling.

He was a smart-looking man, with average height, wearing a classic shirt and formal blue trousers. He seated himself on the only chair facing all the others. 'I am your Mentor Michael Bolt, and welcome to the Class of Introduction, in attendance of all the four Grading groups' Freshers every year,' he said, 'Before we begin, it is my duty to ask and clarify any doubts or uneasiness you may have. Please speak up and clear your mind of any queries you have right now, because I need a fully attentive class.'

Surprisingly, nobody said anything.

'Okay, then. Today, you all will be learning about what, how and through what medium, you are going to be imparted knowledge of the supreme Realm Power. About the question of how… I think our principal has cleared that. Now, you need to know about what all you'll be learning. First of all, I must warn you all that you must not get too excited, for this is no extraordinary school teaching you about the so-called *magic*,' Mentor Bolt began, pacing around the room, using air quotes for specific words. 'You will have subjects integrated with essential science and Mathematics concepts. This is just like school on Earth, but has Realm Power integrated in the course. In my classes, you will be learning about theories of science and how those concepts are overruled using RP. In Mentor Vijay's classes, you will be learning Practical Application Skills, that is to say, physical education integrated with learning how to make friends with your Majenimals and using your Articles of Power for certain purposes. There are various other classes, which I neither have the time nor the patience to mention right now. Another important fact you all ought to know is that in my first official class, I will put some invisible control bands on your Articles of Power and Majenimals, if you have any. This is to prevent misuse of RP until you all are of age to qualify as an adult Sternindian, which is twenty.'

As he said that, Alex heard some loud sighs from others, who were obviously expecting something else.

He resumed, 'Now, you all must know about the medium through which you are going to be educated. There isn't any object other than your Article of Power which may come in handy. For all the organisms of the three realms, the hand is the main weapon. Let's understand with the help of an example. When you don't have a weapon, you use your fist, that is, your hand. When you don't have a tool, you use your hands for doing work. So, even though the hand is the main tool, it isn't all that helps in one's adaptation to the use of Realm Power. Along with the Supporters and the hand—precisely, the *palm* of the hand, the fingers are main source of power. When you use your hand to hold something or do some work, you mostly use your fingers to grip the object. There are many more applications that signify that the importance of fingers is more than that of the hand. You don't use a wand, or a staff, or anything to wield power. You use your fingers. In fact, the wands and the staffs manufactured in Sternind are only for differently abled people, and they are half as efficient as your own fingers. So, be grateful that you have a hand, or you would've had to use a stupid wand. Also, even when you are listening to me talk about all "supernatural" things, don't think that you'll be playing with fire, or orbs of electricity with your fingers. That's all in stories. We Sternindians talk about real life. All you need to know is that Realm Power is invisible, and it is the support of each and every organism of the two realms.'

Someone raised a question, 'Why is it not for the third realm's people? And what *is* the third realm?'

'You need not know *what* is the third, but all I can tell you now is that the inhabitants of the third realm don't think of Realm Power as a support, but they misuse it to think of it as their servant and slave,' replied Mentor Bolt.

Alex understood what Mentor bolt said, and kept it in mind. Though his excitement was lowered by learning about the basic subjects, he decided to get on with it. There was no turning back now.

'Ahem,' said Mentor Bolt. 'Now, I guess you all don't have your notebooks with you, do you? Very well, then. I must also notify you that you all have to buy your books and notebooks until tomorrow morning, for the official session is going to start then. So, with this final word, I end this class of introduction. Good day, Freshers!' He went out of the classroom, and as soon as he departed, the chairs, desks, walls and pretty much everything else dissolved into thin air. Alex and some confused looking Freshers were left standing in the misty corridors again.

Alex checked his timetable again. The next class was in the Practical Application Skills' grounds with Mentor Chakravarti. Just as he looked up from his booklet, Alex saw Lester, Kevin and Angelina coming towards him.

As they drew nearer, Alex noticed the weird expressions on their faces. Lester looked so glum it made Alex wonder whether someone had recently forced sewer water into his mouth. Angelina arrogantly said, 'Hi, see ya later!' before going away without a second look. Kevin, who was assigned to Fate, wore a dark blue and red outfit and had a **Why did you do this to me?** look on his face. As Alex addressed them, he figured that Kevin was still mad at Clairon, and Lester was bummed that there wasn't much special in learning Realm Power. He said that 'it did not meet his expectations'. 'Well, that justifies it. See you guys later,' said Alex, as Lester and Kevin went away.

Alex was still worried about Angelina. What if... what Lester had said *was* true? Maybe Cloedboriogd was controlling some part of Angelina, and making her so arrogant and selfish, that she would be angry at her friends all the time and walk away without giving them a second look. If that was true, Alex needed to be on the lookout, and try to get Angelina to understand it all. He just hoped that he wouldn't get an offensive reply from her.

Waving off the thought at the moment, he started looking forward to the next class.

Alex had considered locating the Practical Application Skills' (PAS) grounds, but had decided against it after having a look at the booklet of timetables. It clearly stated the way to each PAS ground according to when and where one was supposed to be. He located the elevator once again and hit the "FLOOR 109" button. When the elevator doors parted, sunlight hit his face. He was amazed when he saw how reality had been bended; how an open-air ground was located in a multi-storeyed building. Before him stretched another grassland, populated with patches of beautiful flowers here and there. He was elated by such a sight; there was no limit of the expanse; it was endless; the thought of studying, of even *being* in such an environment – A *natural* environment – lifted his spirits. This was unlike normal schools, even though it seemed familiar. School on Earth didn't have endless grounds; the classes didn't take place in such a pleasant place, they were conducted in boring, small and closed classrooms.

To be at such a place was truly an exhilarating experience for Alex.

Looking around, he noticed that most of the students around him were older than him, taking his *the-then-teen-age* into view. Maybe… it was rare for a fresher to get into Determination; maybe students had a chance to be in Determination only in their second year. Angelina seemed right… Maybe suffering *was* what awaited Alex…

Trying to get rid of thoughts of Angelina and her useless predicaments, he started looking through the crowd, searching for someone who looked as troubled as he was. But no such luck. He decided to worry about his problems later and focus on the class, which was about to start.

Suddenly, Mentor Chakravarti walked out of the elevator and approached the others. He raised himself up in the air like he had done earlier, and said, 'So, let's see who we have here. Hmm… A bunch of freshers and all my old students. It's good, then. First thirty minutes of this class are dedicated to the Freshers, and other students will be addressed later. So, let us begin!'

The older students formed a queue that headed towards a certain area of the grassland – at an awfully fast speed – and soon disappeared. Alex wondered what they did in their free time, but realized that he had to focus on Mentor Chakravarti.

'Freshers, as this is your first class, I'll be starting with the basics of using your Supporters. So, everyone, grip your Supporters firmly, and observe them carefully,' he said. Alex took out his Primo and gripped it firmly in his hand. Many people looked surprised at its sight, but Mentor Chakravarti paid no attention. He continued, 'You see, Supporters are not your *tools*, and won't work according to you. They'll only help you when *they* feel you need help. Even though these are inanimate objects, they have minds of their own, all thanks to the large quantity of Realm Power stored in them. So, in order to gain their support and be their friend, you will have to keep them happy, comfortable, and entertained. And by this I don't mean that you have to decorate them with all sorts of fancy material like glitter and be done with it. I mean to say that you have to keep faith in them and keep them in a good environment. You'll have to clean them daily, just like a champion shines his beloved trophies. And most of all, you'll have to develop your love for them, and trust them, not just consider them as assets to keep you out of danger.'

Without waiting for a second, he spoke up again, 'And, I must remind you that my classes have two objectives. One, the care of Supporters, and two, physical fitness. Speaking of physical fitness, now, you all must do twenty push-ups, two planks and fifty sit-ups within the time limit, that is, twenty minutes. So, your time starts now!'

The class soon ended for Freshers, and Alex checked the timetable again. The next fifteen minutes were free for Determination and Hard Work Grading Groups. Alex decided to head to the boys' dorm, hoping to find Lester there.

On reaching there, he found Lester leaning against a wall, studying his timetable intently. 'Let's see what we have here,' Alex said as he addressed Lester.

'Hmm? Oh, yeah. Hey,' Lester said but kept staring at his booklet.

'Dude, you're scaring me. That's just a booklet. You look like you're gonna tear it apart like a wolf,' Alex replied.

Lester tossed the booklet away frisbee-style, turned towards Alex and said, 'It's nothing much. Was just engrossed in it `cause I'm shocked that school, *the school* has started again. Just naming some place that imparts education *Institute* doesn't mean it is different from school. I'm feeling bound to homework again. That… that *burden* is here again.'

'Just take it lightly, man,' Alex said as he placed his hand on Lester's shoulder. 'I have also thought about this, and have got over it. Now there's no turning back.'

'You're right, I guess.'

Right then, Alex's access card started vibrating. It formed an image in his mind, depicting Angelina trying to get into the dorm. 'Hey, Lester, I think Angelina's wanting to meet us. Let's go see her.'

'Okay. These access cards are quite tricky. You know, I was just trying to say what you said right now before you said it. Do you get what I am trying to say now, though?'

'Yes. I mean no. Let's get going.'

As Alex and Lester went out of the dorm, they found

Angelina standing a few feet away, gesturing at them to come towards her. She said, 'So, you know, I've discovered an amazing thing. I was with Clairon the other day, you know, since we both are assigned the same GG and all. We got to know that *you* get to *choose* which class you need to attend- Practical Application Skills' or Shape Shifting classes. They say that only a handful of people are capable of accomplishing the task of Shape Shifting, so the teachers don't exactly jump on the idea of telling Freshers about this choice. You can only opt for Shape Shifting if you know about it, and the only way to do that is ask the Mentors about it. I was really getting bored of Mentor Vijay, his… Weird attitude. So, I asked him about any alternative to his subject.'

'Didn't he kill you that very moment?' asked Lester mockingly.

'He sure *did* give me a murderous look. Not bragging, but I gotta say it took guts to ask him, after only hearing some rumours about such a choice of subjects. I'm feeling like… I'm being… Rational. But it feels good! Feels like some great power is fuelling me from within,' replied Angelina.

Alex was scared, which was evident from his expression. Lester might also have sensed the presence of Cloedboriogd in Angelina. He was looking like he would run away screaming "Mommy!" anytime.

'Anyway,' Angelina continued, 'I've decided to go for Shape Shifting. I have a feeling I'm gonna excel in it. Will you two come with me?'

'Um… Well, I…' Alex hesitated a bit. Lester stayed quiet.

'What? Don't tell me you aren't *enthusiastic* about it,' Angelina said, giving special emphasis to the word "Enthusiastic", almost in an angry tone.

Before Alex could say anything, she continued in a louder voice, 'I knew it. Cloedboriogd was right. You both don't think of me as your friend. You are not my friends. You think of me as a stupid fellow who follows you *TWO* BEST FRIENDS!'

'No, Angelina. Listen–'

'No! I don't want to hear anything from you. It would be better if you two ungrateful cheats don't approach me or talk to me, or I will–' Suddenly Angelina's voice changed to the same male voice Alex had first heard when she had turned into a demon at Wasor—The demon Cloedboriogd. '–KILL YOU!' Angelina aka Cloedboriogd ended as she turned into a demon, sprouted large black wings and flew away into the mist.

Lester turned towards Alex, terrified, 'Dude. –'

'–Cloedboriogd,' Alex finished, aware of the danger and suffering that awaited them.

Chapter 8

Peter Colter

'What I just saw is beyond my understanding,' said someone shrouded with mist. It was hard to make out who he was.

Alex and Lester were standing there, shocked, just as Angelina had been possessed by Cloedboriogd again. 'Who's there?' Lester called out.

Mentor Chakravarti appeared out of the foggy surroundings, and said, 'I noticed everything that happened here a few moments ago. I think this is beyond my understanding, and I feel it is very important. That wasn't your Majenimal, was it? Surely this is a serious matter. I'm going to talk to the principal about this and finalize a meeting time for you and him. You'll need to tell what you make out from this incidence, and speak only the truth. Otherwise, punishments can be harsh. Now, go. Your classes are starting. And I'll be watching both of you closely. And that monster girl also, whoever and wherever she is.' He then walked ahead, towards the elevators – normally – as if nothing had happened.

'I can't understand how these teachers remain calm all the time,' said Lester.

'Me too. I wish I could be like him,' replied Alex.

'Yeah.'

'But now, let's get to class. We can't do anything about what happened right now. We'll worry about all this later.'

'Okay, then… I'll be on my way. See you later,' said Lester as he closed his eyes, waited a few moments, opened them again and hurried off in a particular direction.

Alex checked his timetable again. The next class was "Realm Geo". He located the class through his imagination. It wasn't hard to find out where it was, because a large number of different kinds of vegetation and the clear words REALM GEO could be seen by Alex when he scanned the building's first floor. He soon reached the classroom and seated himself, still thinking about how easily Cloedboriogd had taken over Angelina, and how he was going to explain all this to Vishwaroopaha.

A moment later, the teacher came into the classroom, introducing herself as Mentor Kate Smith. She told everyone that the first half of the class would be for the Freshers, but the older students also had to remain in the classroom. Subsequently, she said while addressing the Freshers, 'Here, I'll be teaching you all about a very important sphere of Sternind, and the other realms.

Known as Geography on Earth, I'll teach you all about the major landforms, society, climate along with Realm Power's origin and way of operating. So, today, I'm going to tell you the basics. See, Realm Power is invisible, and it is the energy, the force, that surrounds us. Every organism of the realms can learn how to make use of Realm Power. Someone who has not been given proper training on how to utilize Realm Power *has* definitely used it at least once before, though unaware. You know that thing, that feeling, which you call instinct and gut? That is what and how Realm Power helps you. To make good use of it, just imagine Realm Power everywhere, around you, inside you, and stretched to faraway lands, and ask it for advice each time you find yourself in trouble. It is the greatest helping hand and will surely aid you. Realm Power is like air, since its physical form has never been ascertained. It is spread out to every nook and corner of all the realms, and is helping everyone in one way or another. It is the thing, the concept, that makes us Sternindians and the inhabitants of the third realm different from the residents of Earth. Even though Realm Power is the main core and source of Sternind, it couldn't have developed into a helpful force if not combined with science and knowledge from ancient Sanskrit texts. So, as I have told you half of the basics and before moving on to the next concept, I would like to enquire whether any of you have any questions?'

As soon as she stopped talking, Alex truly realized how silent the room was.

Mentor Smith chuckled and continued, 'I understand your bafflement. Anyway, let's continue. Sternind is one country, divided into states called Prants. Much like early India and Greece, each Prant has a leader, a king. Though everyone accepts the fact that Sternind is one country, there is no love and unity among people; they take advantage of the division of the states and think of their Prants as their territories; their kingdoms. Our Prant is the one which keeps the nearby Prants, or maybe even the whole of Sternind loosely knit together, and acts as the lifeline of Sternind, preventing widespread chaos. It is called "The Heart". It is a peaceful Prant, with no leader and all thanks to dynamic administration, no conflicts. But, if anyone needs any political advice or statistics, they go to the principal of SIRP. Sternind has always been in a state of conflict and crisis since the time when the Savage Person provoked *the-then-united-Sternindians* to wage wars for supremacy.'

The familiar boy, to whom Vishwaroopaha had silently given the responsibility of preparing and handing over the list of people for whom the lodging arrangements had to be made, stood up. He asked, 'But who is the Savage Person? I'm going nuts trying to figure out his identity!' Suddenly, a mischievous smile spread on his face.

Was this guy joking? Alex thought everybody knew little about the Savage Person. Plus, the way he had formed the sentence… It almost seemed like a prank, a joke. He was acting as if everybody knew everything about the *so-called* Savage Person—all the while questioning his own words.

'Please don't try to create trouble and confusion here, Mr Peter Colter. You are known to be a natural troublemaker, aren't you?'

Peter, Alex's arch-enemy from Florida – the one who had bullied and beaten him on his birthday – smiled again and said, 'So I've been told.'

Suddenly, Mentor Smith increased her voice pitch and said, 'Get out! You're dismissed from the class!'

'You're gonna pay for that, you ________!' said Peter in his usual arrogant and abusive tone and stormed out of the classroom.

Alex was suddenly reminded of Peter Colter's nature. He was an abusive brat, who considered himself superior, and most of all, loved fights and beating people. He liked shedding blood from just one punch. He was the one who even bullied other bullies' bullies.

Mentor Smith was certainly fazed by Peter's behaviour, and called out to him as he was leaving the room, 'I'm planning your sixteenth meeting with the principal. Hope you get expelled this time!'

Peter grumbled under his breath and went away without looking back.

Suddenly, Mentor Smith cried in pain and crumpled to her knees. As Alex and some other Freshers rushed to aid her, they saw blood oozing from her face, nose and eyes. Her body was turning blue and fragile; and surprisingly, it appeared as if her bones were also disappearing. Soon, she stopped moving. She wasn't dead; her breathing continued, but it seemed as if she was lifeless.

A moment later, Mentor Bolt appeared through his usual laser-appearance – which Alex thought was just a big show-off – and said, 'Just happened to pass through. You know, that boy Peter is really nasty. And, you all have to promise me that nobody will say anything to anyone about what happened here. It's not that I am saving Peter from trouble, but it's just… A very deep and dangerous matter, which you all can't possibly comprehend. If you break your promise, I guess this will be *your* condition next.' He gestured towards Mentor Smith, who lay on the ground.

'But will she be fine?' Alex asked.

'Oh, you bet. She'll be alright in a few days. It was just… uh, a *misuse* of Realm Power,' Mentor Bolt replied as he lifted Mentor Smith, who was as flexible as jelly now. Then Mentor Bolt headed out of the classroom, giving one final warning to everyone, '*Don't* gossip about this and *don't* forget to get to your next class on time.'

Alex was truly shocked by all the facts and questions that had been revealed. He surely needed their answers, and the person who could help with that had to be—Vishwaroopaha. Alex had to meet him right then, no matter what. He was *not* going to attend any classes until he knew what was going on. He decided to head towards the principal's office.

He scanned the building, located Vishwaroopaha's office and ran to get there, even though it was quite a long distance. The office was located in a section of SIRP perfectly visible without the required usage of Realm

Power. Surprisingly, Vishwaroopaha himself was leaning against the door of his office and gazing somnolently towards the misty doorway Alex had come through, as if just waiting for him. Lester too unexpectedly showed up there a few seconds later. As it turned out, despite Mentor Bolt's warnings, word about the tragedy of Mentor Smith had travelled fast, and having heard it, he had also decided to meet Vishwaroopaha. Such a sight shocked Alex, where Lester was looking tense and Vishwaroopaha was in his usual calm but annoying state, waiting for them.

Opening the door to his office, Vishwaroopaha said sternly, 'Come in.'

It was a normal room, with piles of papers in a corner, and a rectangular table hosting a mug of coffee surrounded by two uncomfortable wooden chairs at one side and a comfy recliner at the other. Alex and Lester seated themselves on the wooden chairs, but Vishwaroopaha remained standing. He started pacing up and down the room, and said, 'I know what's popping up in your mind. A bunch of questions, right? You want to know about Cloedboriogd, Angelina's cure, why did your Supporter catch my eye, and why did I ask you about any problems in SIRP, and about Peter, right?'

Alex was left speechless. This was the exact summary of the questions left in his mind. All he could manage right then was 'Right' when he realized his voice was cracking, and his throat was dry.

'So, let's start with the last question. I asked you

all about any problems here because I feared that you might've had a run-in with Peter, your enemy from Earth who is also a Sternindian. Now you might be thinking how someone so underserving from Earth was chosen as a Sternindian. The thing is, we, the mentors of SIRP, also don't know why. All we know is that that boy is dangerous, mysterious, and not disciplined at all. We better keep our distance from him and let him do his work, because we don't know who he is and how powerful his family or relations are. We don't want any conflicts and will always be peaceful, until we really feel the need to resort to violence. Meanwhile, we are being silent, and not taking any serious actions regarding Peter Colter, much less expelling him. I hope this is clear now.'

'Yes,' Alex replied, keen to know more.

'Next,' Vishwaroopaha continued, 'I would like to tell you that all your other questions are connected. I will give you the answer to them in a few moments, but you must stay calm, and take in the information I will be providing you without any questions. This is the best deal I can offer.'

'Deal,' Lester said, easing the expression on his face a bit.

Alex also calmed down, and started listening attentively.

'It all started a few centuries back,' Vishwaroopaha said, 'when Cloedboriogd, the Majenimal of the Savage Person and his master, started creating disunity among Sternindians. The wars started, and the Savage Person escaped from the chaos, unnoticed. Later, the people of our Prant, including me, became aware of his plan. We somehow managed to stop his Majenimal, the vicious Cloedboriogd from escaping. We chained him using the original mythical Primo, actually two copies of it, which possessed its original characteristics and power. We also enchanted his bond further, so that he could not escape Earth until he had both the Primos, in his aid. We figured he would stay there forever, and will never be able to free himself, but we were wrong. He might've got rid of his bonds, which is evident from his recent involvement with you all.'

'Wait, you *knew* about him and Angelina?' Alex asked, bewildered.

'Yes, of course. Don't you think Mr Brown would have told me?'

'Oh, well…'

'One truth which you need to know, is that Alex, your Article Of Power is *not* a cheap copy of the original Primo, it is one of the clones made to imprison Cloedboriogd.'

'Yeah, we know,' Lester said.

Noticing Vishwaroopaha's confused look, Alex said, 'Don't ask how.'

'I think I *do* have an idea how,' Vishwaroopaha replied, looking annoyed.

'It doesn't matter now. What we need to discuss now is the way to cure Angelina,' Alex said.

Vishwaroopaha, still looking as if he was trying to solve a murder mystery, said, 'Fine. According to me, the only option is to get to Cloedboriogd, and secretly sabotage his base and defences, so that me and my team can get there and put him in chains again. We'll torture him long enough to know his plans and free Angelina from his influence. But, there is a big risk. Since he has the other Primo, and is fully trained to use any Supporter himself, he will be an undefeatable enemy. You have to act stealthily. If he gets the first Primo – the real Primo, which is in your robe pocket right now Alex – he will ascend to Sternind, regroup with the Savage Person, and will be the source of doom. And if you're asking why you need to take the Primo with you to Earth even though there is this risk, I need to tell you that this is just the way things work. You won't be a real Sternindian without your Supporters. Your AOP will act as your defence, and there's no denying that. You need to take your AOP with you. Now, before I give you further instructions about this mission, I need you both to be at least a little capable of self-defence, and study in SIRP for the next few weeks. You may also form a team with some of your friends here who wish to be involved in this matter, for it won't be an easy task. Now, as I had stated earlier, I want no questions, instead only the sudden departure of you both from here. Have a good day.'

Alex gripped Lester's hand and quickly went out of the room, only to see a serious Mentor Chakravarti saying, 'Don't turn back,' as he headed into the room.

As they started walking through the hallway, Lester stalled and started inching towards the door of the office through padded feet.

'Wha–?' Alex objected. 'You're gonna–?'

'Yep,' Lester replied. 'Spy. I need more info.'

'Uh– okay.'

Alex, pressed his ear to the office's door. He heard Vishwaroopaha's voice, '–eeson I called you here, Mr Chakravarti, is to ascertain the information you provided me. Are you sure you saw that incident with your very eyes?'

'What makes you think I didn't, you suspicious hell of a Principal?' replied Mentor Chakravarti in a tone higher than Vishwarooapaha's.

Alex heard some rummaging, whispering, silenced thrashing and clattering of objects on the floor. When the noises stopped, Vishwaroopaha's voice came to be heard, 'Don't you dare try that again. You know I am more qualified in academics and well, *manners* than you. *I* deserve this seat more than you, and so I have it. Be thankful I have not revealed the truth about you until now, despite your attempts at betrayal. You may be a teacher of Supporter skills, but I am the jack of all, master of none. Even though I know less than you, I still know more than you. You may have mastered Supporters, but don't you know that I have the knack of both teleportation and shape shifting, which is a task almost impossible for anybody. Now, answer me honestly, why didn't you tell me earlier that Cloedboriogd was freed?'

'Uh, I didn't know, my dear principal,' Mentor Chakravarti said calmly.

'You knew. I know that look on your face when you lie. Don't fib now. I know you don't want to confess. Then I guess I'll have to take drastic measures. Be ready for your doomsday tomorrow.'

'No! Wait. Listen, a few months back, when I got the news about the escape of Cloedboriogd, I also received information about one of the two AOPs. You know that that Fresher Alex's Supporter is one of those two Primos, because Mr Brown said to you that he suspected it, right? But don't you want to know that how did it get there?'

'I do. You may continue.'

'When Cloedboriogd set himself free, he tried to locate both the Primos—The ones you had enchanted to fly far away from Cloedboriogd's reach when he got rid of his bonds. He eventually found one of those, you know, but the other one was retrieved by one of my agents, who presented it to me. I understood all that had happened and gave it to an old uneducated beggar for safekeeping, who didn't have any other Supporters. People usually don't rob beggars, so I thought it would be safe there until he died, and then Realm Power would give it to the right person. Then that boy inherited it, and that is where the AOP is till date.'

'You may go now. I need not give any remark,' Vishwaroopaha said.

As Mentor Chakravarti's footsteps became louder, Alex and Lester ran from there, not knowing whether he had seen them. They soon reached the Boys' dorm and plopped themselves on their beds.

'Whoa, whoa. This exceeds my normal limit of low underground understanding. My central processing unit has some loose wires, and this extra data is starting a spark inside my brain. So, all in all, I'd like to say I am flattered,' said Lester slowly.

'Dude, are you slowly descending into the oblivion of stupidity? All in all, I'd like to ask, are you drunk?' Alex replied in the same manner.

'Hm? Hmm. Hm... Like I said, I am dead. So I gotta sleep. That resets my brain to its factory defaults and lets my limbs work the way they usually do. Good night, `lex!' Lester said and lay down on his bunk bed with a loud thud.

'Was it really that or was it that?' Alex thought, fearing if he himself had started thinking illogically like Lester.

Alex thought about the information he had gained. Apparently, all of this revolved around Cloedboriogd, the Majenimal of the Savage Person, the two Primos, and most of all, the impending doom. But one intuition that Alex could not overrule was that Peter Colter was somehow involved. Coming back to the present, he wondered what was next, apart from the classes.

Suddenly, his access card beeped and Kevin entered the dorm, singing under his breath. 'Hey, whatcha doing there, buddy? How was your day?'

This reminded Alex of something else Vishwaroopaha had asked them to do. Apart from bracing themselves for another deadly adventure, what Vishwaroopaha had hinted Alex was to recruit a team to go with them. Alex decided to start with Kevin, since he looked in a good mood.

Alex told Kevin everything, from the start to the end. 'This is a really nicely cooked up rumour, and I gotta give you credit for such a believable tale you converted it into. But I don't wanna be the victim of your so-called "Epic Prank", thank you very much,' replied Kevin after Alex had finished.

'No, Kevin, it's not like that. That was a thing of the past, the pranks, which I used to do back in school! See, we're not in school, and I'm an adult now!' replied Alex just before he looked at himself, thinking, 'Uh-Oh.'

He then continued quickly, 'Well, I guess we *are* in a new school, and I'm not physically an adult, but my brain is all grown up, Kevin! If you could just trust me on this...'

'And I am supposed to believe this gibberish? No way. I don't have a strip of paper stuck to my forehead with the letters "S-T-U-P-I-D" written on it. Just don't try anything on me, because I assure you, it's not gonna work. You're really irritating at times, Alex,' replied Kevin as he turned away and started walking towards his bunk.

Alex blocked Kevin's way, and stopped him, gripping his shoulder tightly. 'Look into my eyes, Kevin. Do I look like I'm telling a lie? Think about why would I play a prank on you, Kevin. Especially, now, when we are Freshmen here, and know nothing of what this world is. We need to stay together, be friends, and face whatever is out there.'

Kevin smiled. 'Yeah, there really wasn't any need of that pep talk right there. You had almost convinced me to join you a few moments ago. I was just double checking, you know.'

'Dude, I feel like punching you and hugging you at the same time, but I guess I'm not gonna do any of that right now. Come. Let's discuss,' said Alex gesturing towards his bunk bed.

'Not now, bro. I need to get the supplies. You know, books and all. It feels like we're somewhere... Different. I just hope I find a cool place like an Arcade out there,' Kevin said to Alex as he started heading towards the door of the dorm.

'Okay, then, see you tonight. And, oh, could you just do me one more favour?'

'Yes?' Kevin asked, turning back.

'Can you get your sister, Marrisa into joining us? And you know, I'm asking you to get someone else in on the plan because… It feels like we're gonna need one more person. I don't know what we'll have to do, but I guess it's not easy. Plus, getting Marrisa with us won't be tough for you. I mean, she's your sister and you're both in the same Grading Group so…'

'Sure,' Kevin said, giving Alex a thumbs up.

Soon after Kevin was gone, Alex decided to get the school supplies himself. He checked the booklet for places to visit, and found a clear answer—The market.

'Typical,' Alex thought again.

Alex glanced at Lester, who was looking hilarious in

his sleep, smiling and drooling over his pillow, muttering something about "Damn Cloedboriogd" and "Poopy man kicking lamb". To Alex, it seemed that old Lester was as good as he was, rebooting his CPU aka brain to make it more stable.

Alex started off for the market. He scanned SIRP, located the exit, and headed out. The afternoon sun was shining in the sky like a divine orb. He made his way through the streets, asking people for directions. At last, the loud sounds of chattering people and shouting vendors reminded Alex of a street market in India, which he had noticed during his trip a few years back. The Sternindian market didn't seem much different.

The place was not very special, just an ordinary market with extraordinary people, cultures and heritage, whom Alex knew little about. He bought his supplies using the monthly pocket money given to all Freshers of non-Sternindian families.

At last, when he returned to the dorm, he noticed that Lester was waking up from his nap. He asked him to go and get his supplies. As soon as Lester started walking out of the dormitory, Alex took a look at the things he had bought. He had just asked for the basic package of books for a Fresher, and had received a bunch of notebooks, and textbooks.

He frowned. He did not like this. For a moment, he thought that even a hideous place like Wasor Island was better than this… This *school.* He aggressively threw his books on the ground. Frustrated, he realized that he had started liking adventure and danger. His inner self wanted more daring tasks, more bafflement and more thrilling experiences. 'Huh. Weird,' he thought about it as he picked up his stuff and neatly placed it nearby. He was exhausted.

The sun was dipping below the horizon. The surroundings had started getting noisy. Hordes of students were entering the dorm, chatting and laughing. Alex wished he also had someone to talk to. He realized he had two best friends, but only one of them was sane now. Looking at the other students, their happy lives, made him feel more comfortable. Even though he wasn't happy, these people were. At least someone was having fun; not being drowned in sadness and mystery like himself.

He fought the urge to cry. Maybe it was because of his happiness for the people around him, or his sadness of losing Angelina. He tried to keep himself stable, like Lester always did—by cracking jokes. But there was no one to share his humour with. He was feeling the need to be with someone, a companion, be it anybody—A Fresher, a teacher, a guy, a girl.

There was a lot missing in his new life in Sternind. But he decided he had to put a stop to these kinds of thoughts, thinking it would lead to some kind of emotional turmoil inside him. He really needed a break and a good night's sleep, and so he got himself one.

Chapter 9

Pressure is Pressurizing

'Pressure due to studies? Hmm… Ah. Pressure. What an exciting word. Do you know how hard pressure is? How hard and painful it is when it slams you on the cheeks via a transportation method—My hand. Do you, boy?' the Theoreticals teacher Mentor Charlotte Murray said, scolding a boy who had complained about the amount of subjects, syllabus and pressure on the students. She was an old and strict woman, who could make anybody gulp in fear just by the looks of her face.

'N-no.'

'Then shut up.'

'So, as I was saying…' while Mentor Murray continued, Alex's concentration diverted towards something else—About two months had passed since his first day at SIRP. The same routine—Getting up, attending classes, taking notes, returning to the dorm, going out to chat with Kevin, Marrisa and Lester, controlling his clone, studying, being lost in deep thoughts and finally, getting to bed.

A lot of time had lapsed since Vishwaroopaha had asked him and Lester to form a team with their friends for the mission and learn about Sternind and their new life in SIRP. But still, there was no further news regarding the plan from him. Maybe he was waiting for the right moment… *The right moment? For what?* Alex doubted his own thoughts.

The day ended soon. Alex sat down in a common room, lined with many rows of seats. Lester, Kevin and Marrisa arrived a few moments later.

'So, since we're good friends and all now, what'd you guys like me call you?' Marrisa asked.

'Call you? What'd ya mean?' Alex said.

'Aw, you don't have nicknames? Anyone?' she looked around, only to see blank faces.

'Guess not,' Lester said. Kevin nodded.

You ought to have some nicknames! The way close friends call you, using your nickname, makes them different from others.'

'Well, then, you can make up our nicknames,' Kevin said.

'Trust me, you're not gonna like them,' Marrisa replied, smiling.

'Ah, whatever. Let's just get this over with,' Lester said.

'Fine, then. So, you see Alex is a nickname in itself, and–'

'Nope. It's not. I'm *not* Alexander.'

Suddenly, the CY device assistant Alexander grumbled in a low voice from somewhere inside Alex's pocket, 'Who? Me?'

Alex whispered back to him, 'Shut up and sleep.'

'Okay, then. If Alex isn't a nickname, we can go with Nerdy Donkey.'

'*What*? That's ridiculous!'

'Warned you won't like 'em. But now, you're stuck with this nickname forever.'

'I'm not.'

'You *are,* Nerdy Donkey,' Lester said.

'Mm-Hmm. There's nothing you can do about it now, Nerdy Donkey,' Kevin added.

Alex expression right then was both murderous and hilarious.

'So, as we move on to Lester, we're gonna call you–'

'Grrrr,' Lester said.

'What? A dog?'

'No. *GRRRR.*'

'What does that mean? What's its spelling?'

'You know what, just forget it. I'm happy with Lester.'

'Alright, then. We'll have a hilarious one for you, for sure. Just wait until I come up with the perfect one.'

'So, Kevin–' Marrisa looked around. 'Kevin?'

Kevin had bolted, and had indeed done the right thing. 'Smart guy,' Alex said.

Now, Alex realized that it was time for Marrisa to get roasted. He said, 'What's your nickname, Marrisa? Puffy fluffball?'

'What? I didn't–'

'Puffy fluffball,' Lester grinned.

'Puffy fluffball,' repeated Alex.

'Yeah, right. Puffy fluffball,' Kevin came from nowhere and sat down next to Marrisa.

'You don't dare–' Marrisa tried to interrupt.

And then, the chorus sang in her ears, for Alex, Lester and Kevin had started shouting and singing the name in a hilarious tune. A few moments later, Marrisa walked away in embarrassment, rolling her eyes.

The boys burst out laughing.

'Ha! That was fun!' Kevin said.

'Someday, I'm gonna compose a mock song with this title.'

'Good luck with that,' said Vishwaroopaha as he appeared out of thin air, with an annoyed expression on his face. 'You really don't feel ashamed of mocking someone older than you? Your own friend? And Kevin, she's your sister. This shows that you're not fulfilling your duties as a good brother.' Kevin frowned, like Really?

'We were just having fun,' said Lester childishly.

'Why are *you* here, anyway?' Alex asked Vishwaroopaha.

'To give you all further information about the plan. But first, we need to have Marrisa here. And that must be done by Kevin, for this is the chance when he can prove that he's a good brother. Right?' said Vishwaroopaha, looking at Kevin.

'Whatever,' Kevin said and walked out of the room, looking annoyed.

'Having fun with your friends?' Vishwaroopaha asked Alex after a long silence and a staring contest, as if to judge whose stare was angrier.

'Not much without Angelina,' Lester said.

Alex gave him an expression, like, Really, man?

'Ah, I understand your grief. But don't worry, we'll finish this soon,' said Vishwaroopaha.

'Considering that we don't fail this "plan", get tortured by Cloedboriogd, let him unite with the savage person when he gets both the Primos, and bring destruction to all the three realms? No, thank you very much,' said Alex.

'It isn't like that, my boy–' Vishwaroopaha had started to say when Marrisa came back with Kevin, talking and laughing.

'So… You're not mad?' Lester asked her as she sat down.

'Oh, I am. But that'll have to wait. For now, just chill out, man. And oh, by the way, Kevin's new nickname is–'

Kevin cleared his throat loudly.

'Fine,' Marrisa said, giving him a sheepish look.

'So, I've gathered you all here to discuss the further actions we need to take and finalize when you all should start your quest.'

'Okay. Go on,' Marrisa said, yawning.

Alex started listening attentively. Lester changed his expression from exasperated to flabbergasted. Kevin looked puzzled, but then straightened his face.

Vishwaroopaha began, 'We know that Cloedboriogd is an extraordinarily smart Majenimal, and a Supporter of the Savage Person. He is in control of Angelina, but that is just a part of him—I don't know how or why can Cloedboriogd be at two different places at the same time, but yes, it's the truth. So, his real body, his real soul and presence is somewhere else—On Earth. That is where he had broken free of his bonds, by slowly scratching the tip of the index finger of Alex's Primo, and loosening its grip on him. It was all the fingers of both the wooden hand Primos that were keeping Cloedboriogd in his prison, but when just a *tip* of a finger was scarred, it was enough for him to escape. He then might've used all of his power to get out of the reach of the Primos. We don't have his exact location right now, but we have a hint—It appears that he was seen by one of our spies who conveyed this information to us before being killed by Cloedboriogd. The place where he was seen is... The country India, located in the southern portion of Asia, a continent on Earth. Before getting his soul snuffed out of his body, our spy didn't even manage to tell us in which political state of India that demonic beast was.'

'My head is spinning,' said Lester untruthfully.

Vishwaroopaha ignored him and continued, 'Now, you might be thinking about how to find him in such a large country. See, what you have to do is look out for dangers and visit all the important destinations in India, like tourists. But first of all, check out the area near Cloedboriogd's prison, which is in the Lonar Lake, a great wonder—Sternindian, of course, even though people of Earth think of it as natural. It is located in the state of India called Maharashtra. If you get nothing there, pay special attention to the crime-prone areas. Cloedboriogd will feel the presence of the second Primo, and will find you all by himself,' said Vishwaroopaha.

'So, what do we do next, get ourselves killed?' Lester asked.

'Sort of,' replied Vishwaroopaha. 'You act like you've been caught off-guard on the way back to your home. You have run away from Sternind because you did not feel like home there. You act like you don't know who he is. You say that you think he's a Sternindian, and you want him to forgive you all for trespassing. Beg, kneel, and cry for mercy with pure terror in your eyes at his sight. But don't overdo it, because after the continuous repetitions of your lies, it won't be long till he senses the truth.'

'What if he gets suspicious and asks why I have the other Primo?' Alex asked.

'You have to stay mum on this matter. I repeat—You don't know anything about Cloedboriogd, the Primos, or me and Mr Brown. Well, technically, you only know about me as SIRP's principal. You people are just normal students who did not feel good in SIRP. Again, beg for forgiveness.'

'Just imagine, if he figures out who we are, what we know, snatches the Primo from me, and almost kills us… Then?'

'There is no chance of that, because if he were to

know about you all, he would know everything—Every piece of information about you and your life in Sternind. I had already told you that there is a lot of risk. But you have to free Angelina, right? So, after you fake your identity and convince Cloedboriogd to take you to his…'

'Base? War base?' Lester suggested.

'Place of Killing?' Kevin said.

'His prison? His home?' Marrisa said.

'Yeah, something like that. It's the place where he resides. It might be near his prison, concealed deep down the Earth, or hidden high in the sky. If Cloedboriogd believes you, he will think that are you guys are real geniuses, since you escaped SIRP. And that too when all the teachers were supposedly after you, in order to demolish the unrest and prevent you all from running off. He will definitely want to use you all for some purpose. You need to make some deal, so that he takes you to his base, and maybe even lets you take a peek at his defence systems. Whatever the case is, you all have to break free of his grip, get out of his line of sight and observe the place. Next, you shall sabotage the security systems. Alexander here, Alex's CY device assistant, knows all about Sternindian tech. He will help you all to disable, or at least tweak Cloedboriogd's security systems in our favour. You'll have to complete these tasks in just an hour or two after you get there, otherwise, Cloedboriogd will start getting negative signals from Realm Power, and will personally and painfully kill you. Alexander, are you listening to me?' Vishwaroopaha called out.

Alex's CY device buzzed. He brought it out of his pocket. The screen lit up, Alexander appeared in his Pharaoh costume, saying, 'Yes sir!'

'Okay, so,' Vishwaroopaha replied. 'Alexander, you'll have to inform me about the time when Alex and his friends sabotage Cloedbriogd's defenses. Then, me and my team will be able to enter. You must send a message to my CY device, with the coordinates of the location.'

'Your CY device?' Alex asked.

'Yes. I use it to control Uncle Edward back in Florida.'

'Well, that explains why Uncle Edward is still there in Florida and Vishwaroopaha is right here,' said Lester.

Alex shot him a look like, **How do you know that?**

Lester replied, giving Alex an expression as if to say, **I know stuff**, 'Dude, I spend more time with my CY device than you do.'

'Yes,' said Alexander, 'Our principal does have a CY device. In fact, I love talking to the one who is in there—The cute Alice!' Then he lowered his voice, channelled his eyeballs towards Alex, saying, 'In fact, you know, we are dating!'

'Dude, the volume of this device is conked up to full. We could clearly hear what you said in a supposedly hushed tone right now. And by the way, we don't have any interest in your love life. So, ha-ha and shut up,' said Kevin.

Alexander's face turned red. He said, 'I'm gonna die of embarrassment,' and Alex's CY device automatically turned off.

Vishwaroopaha chuckled. 'That *was* a pun, for sure. Well, if you'd excuse me, I'd like to… uh… Do *things*.'

always try to wriggle away from us when you're done, don't you?' said Lester.

Alex gave him a look like, **You're overdoing it**, which made him relent.

'Why are you doing that?' Alex asked Lester, who had been pacing back and forth for quite a long time now. They were back in the dorm. Kevin had already bid them a good night's sleep.

'It makes me feel better,' replied Lester. 'I'm feeling like a huge 400-pound anvil is resting on my shoulders. It *is* pressurizing.'

'Should I refer to the definition of pressure given by mentor Murray?' Alex replied with a smirk.

'Shut up,' said Lester and sat down on his bunk, head in hands.

'You gotta relax, man. We will get through this just like Was–'

'Enough! I've heard this a lot of times!' shouted Lester. 'How can everything be okay even when you know it's not and never will be? We *won't* be able to GET THROUGH THIS! I have a gut feeling, a feeling that…' Lester's face contorted into a frown, and it seemed like he would cry any moment.

'You know what, Lester? You're just being negative,'

replied Alex in a low voice. 'You see, we do have some good things in our life, don't we? This is just the age of suffering, you think. But it isn't so. We can and should look on the bright side. If we do so, we will automatically forget the dark side. We have increased our lifespans, Angelina will get okay soon, and we'll kick Cloedboriogd's butt so hard he won't even dare sit anywhere.'

'Thank you, Mr *make-someone-speechless*,' said Lester, a smile twitching at the corner of his mouth.

'That is whom I call the real Lester. Now go to sleep, young man. We've got a lot to do tomorrow,' replied Alex.

'*Tomorrow*?' said Lester, bewildered.

'Well, yes. We have to start this tomorrow. The sooner, the better. We'll be on our way as soon as we inform Vishwaroopaha about our departure.'

'This is the second time I am saying this to you, I absolutely don't regret it, and I'm serious—You're crazy.'

'I can't argue with *that* now,' said Alex with a smile, and let his head free-fall on the pillow.

Chapter 10

In for Goosebumps

Alex woke up, yawning. Looking around, he saw neither Lester nor Kevin in the dorm. 'Might've gotten up early, with the stress and all…' he thought. He freshened up and headed out for breakfast on Floor 203. He had decided to call it "Floor 203" rather than the much disliked word "Assembly Hall".

He found his friends hogging the PIZZAS FOR NEWBIES stall.

'So, what do we do, just enter a portal or something, get to India, and be a Rambo and all?' Marrisa asked.

'Seriously, sis? Didn't you hear what the principal had said?' Kevin replied.

'That's boring.'

Alex gave her a **Really?** look.

'I'm goosebumpy,' Lester said.

'That was really lame, bro,' Alex said.

'Sorry, uh… I tend to do that when I'm nervous, especially when I am going on a hide-and-seek expedition with a demon. Especially when I'm going to be handed my head by him.'

'You're overdoing it again,' said Alex.

'I *can't* help it.'

Alex soon realized the problem. His team was nervous, not ready for this kind of thing at all. He had to do something to uplift their mood before they could get going. Something clicked him.

'Hey, Puffy fluffball, what's going on?' he said.

'That kind of rhymed, Nerdy Donkey,' replied Marrisa.

'Grrrr says rrrrr,' said Lester.

'I better not reveal this…' said Kevin.

'But you will have to, Kevin-the-trash-bin,' said Marrisa.

Lester made the most intense "Ew" face Alex had ever seen.

'You know what, this is the lamest of the lamest nickname I have ever heard,' Kevin said.

'Or had,' added Alex, receiving a few chuckles.

Alex's nickname idea had worked a bit, but wasn't enough, for his friends started appearing gloomy again.

'Let's play a game. Maybe that'll make you all feel better. Follow me,' said Vishwaroopaha in an almost commanding tone, who had just arrived and walked straight from the Elevator to where Alex and his friends were. He gestured them to follow him. Soon, Alex found himself standing in Vishwaroopaha's office, which was now clean, and no longer looked like the unmaintained shack of an old man. The piles of papers were neatly arranged in a corner, the dust had been swept off the floor and the furniture, and the best thing which added to the new beauteousness of the room was the group of lantern-like lamps, the glow of which mesmerized Alex's senses. The crappy old chairs and the office table were removed. A few cushioned chairs had been added, and were surrounding a big round table. On it was a board-game's box simply titled "The Run". To Alex, this place seemed truly fit for a game in the evening, given the amazing new lighting situation.

Vishwaroopaha said, 'Please be seated,' gesturing towards the chairs, as he opened the box of "The Run". 'The widely played board game – Ludo, or Parcheesi – as you Americans might call it, was made by taking inspiration from Indian board games. So, *we* Sternindians have developed another version of this exciting game, which is neither Indian nor Western. It is wholly Sternindian. It is very much like Ludo, but has many variations,' he said, flattening the board on the surface of the table.

Alex figured he had just been somewhat grounded into playing such a boring game. Or so he thought.

'So, let's start now,' said Lester. 'And get over with it quickly,' he tried to add under his breath, but they were sitting so close that Alex could clearly hear his words.

'Ah, but before that, you know, just for everyone's

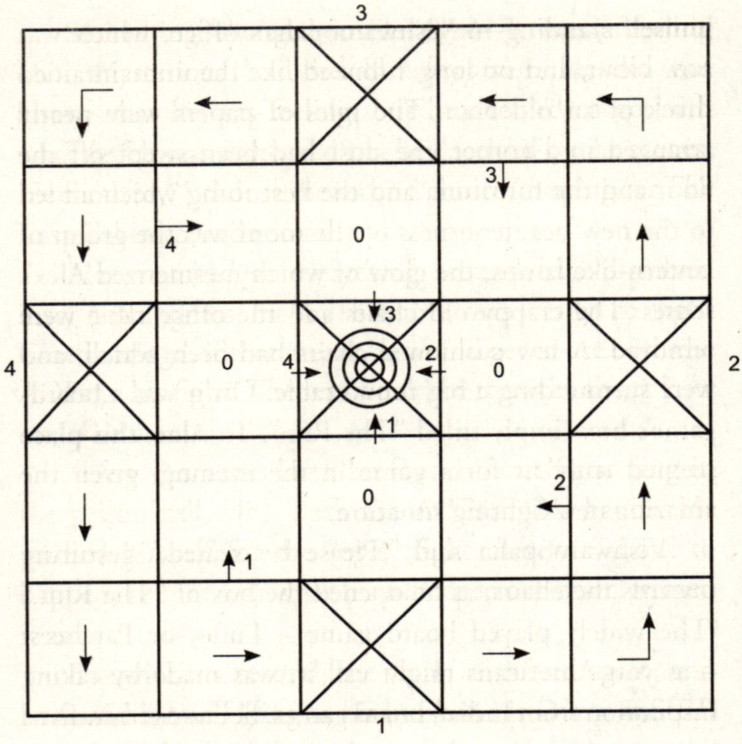

convenience, I should list out the rules, shouldn't I? And also, this game can be only played by four people, so–' Vishwaroopaha was interrupted by Lester, who immediately said, 'I'm outta this, then.'

'I'm sorry, Mr Watson. The situation demands *you* playing the game. I'll stay out of it and help each one of you get the hang of it. Now, listen to the rules,' said Vishwaroopaha. Then, pointing towards various parts of the board, he started explaining the game. Alex memorized its summary–

The Inner ring-

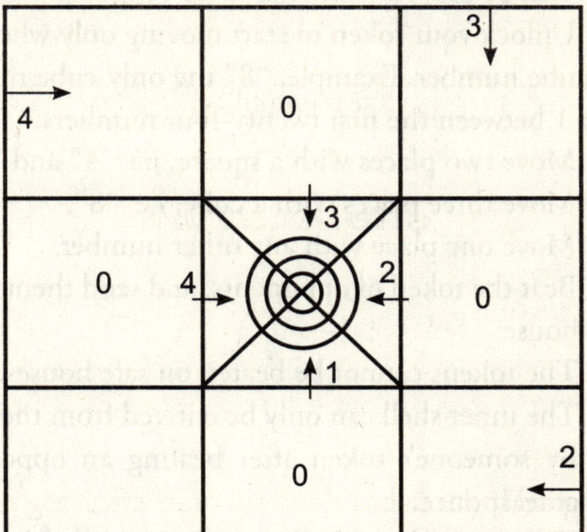

Home House, the place where four locked tokens are kept-

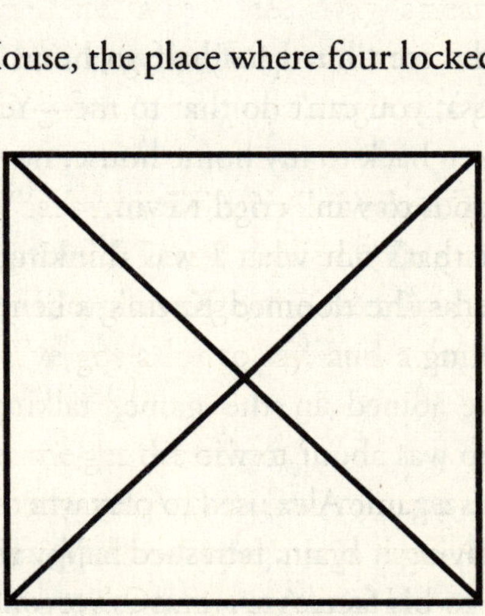

- Play with two dice and four tokens for each player.
- Can be played with two, three or four players.
- Unlock your token to start moving only when you get a cube number. Example: "8" the only cube number except 1 between the first twenty-four numbers.
- Move two places with a square, i.e. "4" and "9".
- Move three places with a cube, i.e. "8".
- Move one place with any other number.
- Beat the token of opponents, and send them to the home house.
- The tokens cannot be beaten on safe houses.
- The inner shell can only be entered from the entry point by someone's token after beating an opponent's token at least once.
- Race to reach the bullseye, or the finish spot. One whose tokens reach the bullseye before all others is the winner.

The game continued for half an hour. 'No, no, no! Okay, Marissa, you can't do that to me—Yeah, no, don't send my token back to my home house, now. Aw man… I was just about to win!' cried Kevin.

'Ah, but that's not what I was thinking, you know,' said Marrisa as she doomed Kevin's token to his home house, laughing.

Everyone joined in the game, talking and often guessing who was about to win.

Ludo was a game Alex used to play when he was really little. But playing it again, refreshed happy memories and brought joy to his face. Apparently, everyone was having fun, too. Their solemn faces had changed into jolly ones.

Vishwaroopaha had truly been successful in changing everyone's mood.

Suddenly, Alex's attention drifted from these thoughts to a weird sensation spreading from his right hand to his brain. It soon morphed into pain. It felt as if molten lava was flowing in Alex's veins. His hand and body started to glow red, and he screamed in pain. The experience was too frightening, and he felt as if he would die of fear sooner than pain.

A few seconds later, through blurred vision, he saw Vishwaroopaha pointing his hand towards Alex's pocket. His pain subsided, and he found his Primo far away from his right hand, lying on the floor. Alex realized what had happened—The weird sensation and pain was inflicted through his AOP. He didn't remember when he had gripped it with his right hand, but he had surely been aware of the pain. Vishwaroopaha had jerked it away using Realm Power, and thrown it onto the ground.

Vishwaroopaha explained, 'It seems that Cloedboriogd is trying to sense the location of your Primo, Alex, by using the other one he has. He cannot do that until and unless you are letting it touch your body. Alex, he might be using your memories to check where your Primo is, so that he can gauge who and where you are. If he succeeds in this process – which he will have to continue for about twenty seconds – he will know everything about you and your AOP, leading to our failure. So, from now on you should make every attempt to not let him take control of your memories using the AOP. And the way you can do that is by not letting your skin touch your Primo. You must conceal this AOP in your pocket at all times, and not instinctively hold it in your hand like you did just now. You may only use your Primo if and when you are in a dire need—Maybe against Cloedboriogd, if the situation persists. He won't be able to get hold of your memories then and there because he will have to concentrate a lot for it, and you can easily beat him if he concentrates on something else other than the fight if and when you both are face-to-face. The matter is getting more and more complicated, and if this team is not ready to face it, we can't win. So, cheer up, and be prepared. You may depart for India today itself. I'm very serious about this, and please don't take my words lightly.'

'Okay, then,' said Lester, rather optimistically contradictory to his new depressing attitude.

Soon, they finished the game with Marrisa as the winner and Vishwaroopaha bade them good luck. Marrisa promised to meet the boys just outside SIRP in an hour as she headed out to the Girls' dorm.

The three boys were lounging in their bunks. 'Dude, how are we gonna get to earth? Ask Mr Brown or something?' asked Lester.

It struck Alex. How could he forget to ask Vishwaroopaha about this?

He decided to not bother Vishwaroopaha now. *Like, who needed another one of his boring lectures?* Alex thought. They would directly go to Mr Brown, tell him what they were about to do, and ask for his help in reaching Earth.

There was nothing to do for an hour. So Alex decided to take a nap, knowing he would need a lot of energy later on.

He was woken up by Lester, 'Yeah, man. Just get up, now. We'll really need that stupid head of yours if we're gonna get going.'

Marrisa was just about to get back. But what interested Alex more than starting on their journey to Earth was Lester's hilarious appearance—He was dressed in weird protective gear, a cricket helmet, cricketers' leg pads, and a very heavy-looking black military-grade vest. He couldn't even walk properly, and resembled a penguin when he moved. 'Dude, just give it a rest. Get rid of those things and return them… Wherever you got them from. You're just embarrassing yourself,' Alex said.

'Already figured that out,' said Lester as he waddled away.

Kevin was waiting at the door of their dorm, gesturing Alex to follow him. Alex got ready, quickly grabbed his Primo and shoved it in his pocket, making sure it wasn't touching his skin. He tailed Kevin till they were out of the dormitory, the vast mist spreading all around them. Kevin looked around dreamily for a moment, then finally broke the silence. 'Fascinating, isn't it?'

'Um… Yeah. Yeah?'

'I feel like I'm looking at this place for the last time. Though I've not been here long, but SIRP will for sure remain in my mind forever—Or as long as I live, you know.'

'Well, I *don't* know, alright? *You* know what, Kevin? You're acting really depressed. Just don't think that you're heading to certain death. Think of what we're about to do—It's just like one of the missions you bravely accomplished to become worthy of living in Sternind. You had courage, right?'

'I had it *then*. Not now.'

'Dude, just know that our principal, Mr Crest, or Vishwaroopaha – I honestly don't know what to call him nowadays – had gone a so overboard with telling us the cons of the plan that he didn't understand that he was scaring us. I've realized this, and you must too. It's just a matter of time before everything returns to normal. You know, the *Sternindian-type* normal.'

'Okay, but… What is the point of sending us to Earth, just after calling us *from* Earth? I was looking forward to a nice year in Sternind—Happy and learning. But this…'

'This is the plan, Kevin. You have signed up for it by your choice, and now there's no turning back.'

'But why send us to earth again? I'm kinda suspicious. Couldn't we have somehow created a stimulus that called Cloedboriogd to Sternind, to finish him here?'

'Kevin, Cloedboriogd cannot escape Earth even if he wishes. He can only get to Sternind when he has both the Primos, the twin powerful AOPs,' Alex replied sheepishly.

'Oh,' replied Kevin, apparently feeling like an idiot.

'Don't freak out, and most of all, don't lose your cool. So just chill the hell out, and be ready.'

'I'm here!' said Lester, dressed in his Grading Group's uniform as he joined Alex and Kevin, with a grin on his face. 'Oh,' he added as he looked at the expression on Kevin's face. 'Are we having a serious convo here, Kevin? Just chill the hell out, bro.'

'That's exactly what I said to him,' said Alex.

'Yeah, that's good. And Kevin, don't let me find you cowering around in some corner when we're face-to-face with Cloedboriogd. Or else, I'll be the first one to shove you in his face,' joked Lester.

'Fine. I'll force a smile for now,' said Kevin, truly forcing a fake sarcastic smile.

Alex noticed how happy Lester was, and how he was trying to make others happy too. He prayed this happiness would never melt away, during and even after their encounter with Cloedboriogd.

They started towards the exit of SIRP. Surprisingly, no Mentor stopped or asked them where they were going during teaching hours.

They met Marrisa just outside the main door of SIRP. Alex once again looked back at the tall skyscraper of his Institute, wishing that he would be able to see it again. It seemed… As if he was bidding goodbye to all his known places and things in Sternind, as if he would never able to return. He feared what Kevin was thinking might actually come true. But he knew it wasn't. He believed that their plan would surely succeed.

Luckily, Alex remembered the way to Mr Brown's house, or they might've been roaming around in the streets all day. On reaching there, they witnessed a strange sight. The front door was open, as if waiting for them. Naturally, they went in.

Relaxing on one of the sofas, 'Mmm. Okay…' was all Mr Brown said as he listened to the whole story, and annoyingly, kept thinking for another ten minutes.

'You're gonna say something or should we…?' started Alex but couldn't finish his sentence. He absolutely didn't know how to go to Earth, or do anything else, without any of his friends' or Mr Brown's help.

'Since I had already been informed about the plan by my master, I believe that you guys indeed need my help. Guess I'm ready to escort you people to good ol' Earth, and maybe even grab some of the amazing spicy street food up there in India,' said Mr Brown finally. 'But you'll need to have a lot of stuff prepared if you wanna stay safe, and not hungry like a beggar. You know what I mean, right? You're gonna need *money*, punks. *Money*. That's what'll keep you alive and just fine until you find Cloedboriogd and execute this *brilliant* plan of yours.' He said the word *brilliant* with pure sarcasm.

'So… What're we gonna do? Exchange some Sternindian currency to Indian? Sorry, but we don't have that much time. Any other alternative, or should I punch you in the face right here?' said Lester, a murderous look in his eyes.

'Ah, but you don't need to take such great pains, of course,' replied Mr Brown in his usual calm tone. 'I've already figured that your morale and firm decision won't last long, and you'll want to get it over with as quick as possible. Luckily, I happen to visit India a lot, and coincidentally, happen to have some money, which is called Indian Rupee there.'

'*I don't care* what it's called! Just hand it over and send us off. And don't talk slow like that, you no-good of an assistant!' said Kevin, bursting.

Alex shot him a warning look, like, **Man, don't- Just don't**. He said, 'I'd not dare say that if I were you, Kevin. With all due respect, just shut your mouth for now.'

'I very well appreciate the fact that you understand things, young man,' said Mr Brown with a sly smile. 'Wait here. I'll bring some money for y'all. Hope you have a nice stay there, and don't get killed along the way.' He went into his room, without giving anyone a chance to say anything.

'So, we're gonna book a hotel, visit tourist destinations, eat food and relax, all in order to find some vicious creature and execute a "plan"?' said Lester.

'Yeah. Doesn't make sense. Going on some vacation-like venture, just to ultimately kill a demon,' said Marrisa. 'But I guess that's what needs to be done, right?'

'Seems like this is it,' said Mr Brown as he came back with a credit card, and some cash.

'As for now,' he continued, 'we're gonna go to Earth. Travelling between realms is a tricky thing. There's a proper procedure for that. You can book an appointment with the head of your Prant, then explain to him/her about why you need to travel to another realm, and then get an escort to the realm you wish to go to. Since the supposed head of our Prant is our very own principal and you people have his consent, I will act as your escort. Understand?'

'Yeah, I don't wanna know all this shit, okay? We don't need to get into any formalities and TO HELL WITH YOUR PROCEDURES! You are taking us to Earth, escort or no escort,' said Alex, his temper flaring a bit, too.

Well, if you're too eager to refuse the tea I was about to offer you, then fine. We're going to Earth. Right now.'

'But *how*?'

'You have seen the limit of heights. Now it's time you see the limit of darkness, and... Well, depth. Have you ever wondered what's in the Mariana Trench?'

A sudden cold swept over the room. Maybe it was just Alex, but he could feel that dreadful feeling throughout his body. Why wasn't there an easy way to enter or exit Sternind? Maybe most people didn't want to, and certainly weren't interested about people from Earth finding Sternind. That's why its entries and exits are located at deadly places. But whatever the case, he needed to get himself and his friends to Earth.

'Doesn't the water pressure crush you down there, Mr Brown?' Lester said.

'Let me give you a good piece of advice. Never worry

about science when you're talking about Realm Power,' Mr Brown said, facing Lester.

'Well, what're we waiting for, then? Let's roll,' said Kevin, standing up.

'Okay,' interrupted Alex, 'I get that we're gonna end up deep in the Mariana Trench on earth, but what will act as the exit from Sternind?'

'It's simple. You can warp there from any place, if you know who to ask,' said Mr brown as he gestured to himself, smiling. This annoyed Alex even more.

'Just get on with it,' said Marrisa.

'Follow me, then,' said Mr Brown. He headed upstairs into a room, the one Angelina might've spent the night in when Alex and his friends stayed at his place.

They followed him to a weird looking table that was wrongly curved, with strangely fitted hinges and legs, not to mention it was actually floating and twisting in the air.

'What's this? Some kind of enchanted table? Lets you do magic and stuff?' Lester said.

'Don't ever say the word *magic* again in front of me. And there shall be no further discussions on this topic. Now look at what I'm doing. I expect you all to observe me from now on, in order to learn the method to leave Sternind.'

Mr Brown rotated his fingers in a certain pattern, and suddenly, the ground beneath the table disappeared into an endless black void, which was almost instantly replaced by a deep puddle of water.

'Now, it's simple. You just need to drown,' said Mr Brown.

Lester's expression was undecipherable. Alex was too flabbergasted to form words. Marrisa spoke up anyway, 'You're not serious, are you? And how can I trust the fact that you're gonna send us to Earth, not make us drown right here?'

'Oh, you've linked two unrelated sentences, you know. You *will* drown, but as a result, you will end up on Earth. The only difference between the truth and your thoughts is that you won't die after you drown.'

'Seriously?' said Kevin.

'What my say in this is, just do everything he says, and get on with it. Then get it over with and head back home. I'm getting a splitting headache, I tell you,' said Alex.

'Fine,' said Lester.

Mr Brown jumped into the puddle, and went straight through the ground. He said, 'I'll be going with you, and just to pacify your suspicious mind, I'll drown first.' He dipped his head under the surface of water, and in a few minutes, after lots of air bubbles and almost muted wheezes, his body became lifeless.

In order to inspect the process, Alex instinctively tried to lift Mr Brown's *now-lifeless-and-maybe-dead* body up. But within a few seconds, the body dissolved into pure black smoke.

'Was that his soul disappearing—On its way to heaven?' said Lester, frantic.

'No, sir. Absolutely not,' said Alexander from Alex's pocket. 'He is on Earth now, I'm sure. What I woke up to say is, don't worry about me, boss. My home is waterproof.'

'*No one* was worrying about you, so just shut up and sleep, but don't forget to complete my clone's routine in Florida,' replied Alex.

'Well, that was rude, but yeah, I'll do as you say, boss,' said Alexander as the CY device automatically turned off.

'Are we sure about this?' asked Marrisa.

'Only one way to find out,' said Alex. And trying to be brave, he added, 'I'll go first.'

Everyone nodded. Alex jumped into the puddle, head-first. He tried to calm himself as he drowned—not thinking about death. Being a good swimmer, his instincts kicked in, and he rose up to the surface of the deep puddle once or twice, but then overrode his instincts. As he lost his breath, water started seeping into his nose, quickly trickling down his mouth and throat. It felt like his body was malfunctioning, as if his liver was located where his brain should be, his nose was located where his throat should be, and water was everywhere. As his brain exploded with pain , he lost control of his body, and floated in a big void of darkness before he finally woke up, surrounded by deep salty water in all directions and a glowing portion of the water above him—the portal to Sternind.

He could see many deep sea creatures and aquatic wildlife, along with a few light sources around him. There were various kinds of fishes, many of which had bulb-like biological structures fixed to their bodies, that helped them see in the dark. But they weren't everywhere, so he was partly surrounded by darkness. Thankfully, Mr Brown spotted him. He was pointing a flashlight at him from just a few metres away. As Alex swam towards him, he noticed that his clothes were dry, even though he was surrounded by water—He could breathe in water. Truly, Mr Brown wasn't wrong about the process, even though he hadn't told them all about it.

His friends joined them a few minutes later. Mr Brown said, 'Well, now you know that I wasn't bluffing. Let's whip out our Aviaboards and–'

He was cut off by a shrill roar from behind. As Mr Brown turned back, Alex saw what had caused the sound. It was a large marine reptile, more than four times an average man's size. Its head was somewhat triangular, crocodile-like jaws lining the inner part of its mouth. It had a long, hard and cylindrical body, with scales flashing in and out when it curved. Its fangs were sticking out from the corners of its mouth, which looked permanently stained with blood. It had spikes and oddly placed fins lining all parts of the body, which made it look even deadlier. Alex was caught off guard as it pounced towards them.

Everyone except Mr Brown screamed and swam in all directions. Alex was frightened by the creature's sight. There was no way he was going to fight it.

Alex couldn't believe what he saw next. Mr Brown calmly swam and approached the tail of the furious creature, and disappeared behind the monster at an angle he couldn't see. He partly suspected that Mr Brown won't show up again—He might've been killed by the creature.

But Alex couldn't see any blood. That could mean Mr Brown was safe. He heard a loud but obstructed sound, like a lever being pulled down. The creature immediately became lifeless, as if it was a machine whose switch had just been turned off.

'A handy security guard, you know,' said Mr Brown, as he came back, totally unfazed. 'Guarding the exit to Sternind from insanely curious people.'

Alex was stunned, just as he always was, when he learned new things about Sternind.

'Well, what're you staring at?' Mr Brown asked as he saw everyone's faces when they gathered around him. 'I'm sure you've all had enough of new things by now, haven't you? Well, I still know what you guys feel. You still gotta cope up with horrendous sights, you know. Let's move on now, shall we?'

Mr Brown brought out his Aviaboards—the ones disguised as a bunch of keys. For the first time, Alex wondered why. Was it for convenience, or do Sternindians like keeping things complicated? Whatever the case, Alex decided to brush the thought off.

Half a minute later, they found themselves shooting up in the sky, and successively levelling their altitude for a quick flight to India. Alex hoped they were on Earth, and not in the third realm as a gateway to Earth, for if they were to go through another Ozone hole, he would surely die. He was partly relieved and partly braced about the things to come, as he witnessed the vast expanse of the Pacific Ocean. It was like a dream come true—If the feeling of having their lives on the line and probably dying within the next few days was excluded.

As they rode on their miraculous Aviaboards, Marrisa spoke up, 'I wanna know what that thing was, Mr Brown.'

'I told you, didn't I?' Mr Brown replied. 'A security guard.'

'A normal security guard is not always a large sea monster which tries to kill people, even the ones who made it. We are Sternindians, and we weren't trying to escape Earth through the portal—We came *through* it, right? Also, wasn't this *security guard* made by Sternindians? Isn't it supposed to only target people of Earth? Why did it attack *us*, then? Is there some problem in its programming? If so, why don't Sternindians change it?'

The answer to that is beyond my knowledge. Sternindians have made it, for sure. But... You know, since we have a way to temporarily shut down the Hainosaurus for our safe passage, why alter its characteristics? We, the Sternindians can get away safely. That's all that matters.'

'What did you just say? Hainosaurus? Is it some kind of marine *dinosaur*?' said Kevin.

Mr Brown chuckled and said, 'It's a mythical prehistoric reptile, the Hainosaurus. For the people of Earth, anyway. For us Sternindians, it's a commendable security guard.'

That was enough for Alex. His head had already been hurting pretty badly, and all this talking only made it worse. He said, 'Can we please shut this now? I'm not feeling very well. Seems like... Something is trying to take hold of me.'

'Is it Cloedboriogd? Is that AOP touching your skin again, Alex?' Lester asked, his expression changing.

'No, man. I was just giving an example of how I feel.

It's just this annoying headache that's taking hold of me. *You*, just relax. *I*, will take a break,' replied Alex.

'What break?' said Mr Brown.

'I don't care if I am soaring through air, if the weather's windy or rainy, if I'm standing, sitting or lying. I'm just gonna take a nap here. Also, you'll have to handle the military when you intrude India's airspace. My suggestion is, you should enchant your Aviaboards with some invisibility Realm Power. I'm not gonna be there, I tell you. And while I'm out, Mr Brown, you gotta get those–' He paused, embroidering his next words with air quotes, '"suddenly-appearing-out-of-nowhere-maybe-out-of-the-Aviaboard curved metal plates" to work.'

Mr Brown blinked twice.

'I seriously don't know what those life-savers are called, the ones you used to keep us tightly secured to the Aviaboards when we were gonna enter Sternind the first time.'

'Oh. The buckles, you mean?'

'Great. They're just called buckles. Why was I stupid enough to not figure *that* out?' Alex thought.

He replied, 'Exactly. I'm gonna sleep, but I don't wanna fall off this Aviaboard. You know, that would be really inconvenient.'

Alex dozed off.

Chapter 11

Gotta find him quick...

Alex woke up, not to the warm tropical winds of India, but to the smell of filthy water, which was more like rotten eggs. He observed his surroundings. He was next to a large lake, dark green in colour. He stood up gagging and looked around. He had been lying next to a large lake, the surface of which acted like a mirror for clouds. The lake was surrounded by little vegetation amidst a small area of barren ground.

Alex saw his friends a few feet away from him—kicking stones, talking and occasionally coughing because of the smell. Not sure why, he ran up to them and hid behind large tress to stay out of their line of sight, and listened to what they were saying.

'...still, we're gonna have to do it, right? No matter what this thing smells like, they say that a meteor had crashed here. I don't believe that. Plus, this place has super bad odour, to be frank. It's also some kind of wonder lake. Nobody wants to be here, because of the bad smell and all. You see any tourists here? No. Sternindians are a totally other matter. No one even dares to pry around this place. That might be the reason why Cloedboriogd wants this as his security. It is also where Sternindians constructed his prison—intentionally at a place that was not to be doubted or researched upon by people other than scientists and doctors—this lake, whose smell keeps people away. Maybe he lives underwater, in the same prison, to lower his chances of being caught. I mean, he might be thinking that Sternindians would search for him everywhere on Earth – thinking that he had broken out of his prison, and is hiding somewhere on Earth – while he would freely chill out in his prison,' Lester said.

'So… You're saying that we're gonna have to go in? Dive into that… *thing*? What if Cloedboriogd has turned his prison into a war base? That water is gonna kill me as soon as I touch it, right?' Kevin said.

'No, dummy. It's just simple water inhibited by green Algae. Not green poison. At least that is *something* that the inhabitants of Earth have discovered,' Marrisa said.

'You're acting as if you aren't– *weren't* a resident of Earth,' Kevin commented, only to receive no reply.

'So when Alex wakes up, what we're gonna do is, we're gonna get us some diving gear, if it is even available around here. If not, I guess we always have online shopping. Then, we'll go deep into this hell of a lake and find Cloedboriogd,' said Lester.

'Assuming this is his base, right?' Marrisa said.

'Yeah, it's okay if we *think* that it is his base. It's just a guess. But even if it is his base, according to the plan, we have to accidentally meet him. If we go intentionally into such a place, then how will we prove that we just stumbled upon him? No one just accidentally meets a demon in a filthy crater-formed lake. I mean, the odds are 0.0001 percent of that happening in a normal situation. Precisely, we can't go in there and tryna prove to Cloedboriogd that we just entered a lake that smells like dead rats and swam deep enough to find him, and that too, *accidentally*.' Lester replied.

'Can we prove this point by saying we were attempting suicide?' said Kevin.

'Seriously?' said Marrisa, eyebrows arched.

'Bro, no one who is frustrated with Sternind tries to freaking suicide when he gets to Earth, rather than going back to his family.' Lester said.

'Yeah, I know. I feel kinda dumb now,' Kevin replied.

'Hmm. Even if we get the solution to these problems, how will we prove that we escaped Sternind without anyone's help? How are we going to tell him that we knew where the portal was and were confident enough to use it? And also, how are we gonna make him believe that that portal had opened in India, and we got lost? It actually opened in the Mariana Trench. No one can *accidentally* travel from the Mariana Trench to India, specifically to Cloedboriogd's prison, and swim into such a demon's lair,' said Marrisa.

'There are lots of loopholes in this plan, and I bet they change with every situation. We are on a fool's errand, I'm sure,' said Alex, appearing from behind the trees. He sat on a nearby large rock, disheartened.

'I'm sorry,' he said to everyone. 'I somehow persuaded you guys to come with me on this mission, and now see, what I've gotten us into...' He could not say more. He closed his eyes, head in hands.

Something touched his shoulder, and as he looked up, he saw Lester, who said, 'We landed ourselves into this mess, and we are gonna get ourselves outta it. Let's figure something out, man. We aren't losing hope yet, are we?'

'No, we're not,' replied Alex, smiling, amazed by how changed Lester looked.

'Thanks for the assurance,' Marrisa said sarcastically. 'What's next?'

'I think that we should leave this part now, because it's the one with the most riddles. I mean, let's go and search for Cloedboriogd somewhere else—*anywhere* else. If we still return unsuccessfully, we gotta take a shot at this ridiculous plan, here at Lonar Lake. That's our only hope. We obviously can't go out there unprepared. And by the way, unless any of you here is undercover Einstein, I guess we don't have any other way to wriggle out of this one,' said Alex.

'Okay,' Kevin said. 'Where should we start, then? A mall, maybe? I feel like watching a movie.'

'For your kind information, we're in India, on a

mission. So *please* shut up,' Marrisa said rolling her eyes, with an irritated look on her face.

'I was just trying to make a joke,' Kevin said like a seven-year-old.

'Wasn't funny,' Lester said, receiving a look fromKevin.

Marrisa brought out her phone, and started scrolling through it. A smile crossed her face. She said, 'Got some news of recent crimes. I don't think Cloedboriogd would stay inside a place like Taj Mahal or whatever, so let's forget the tourist spots. Let's start our search from the other places, where murder or theft has taken place in the recent days.'

'I guess those are the places we should *avoid*. There might be investigations or something going on at those. We should go according to time. We gotta check the crime-prone areas off the list. Let's wait up till tonight, and look out for threats to society, and check whether any of them is related to Cloedboriogd,' said Kevin.

'So… You want us to wake up at midnight, be some kind of ghost busters and all? I'm sorry, but I get super scared whenever I watch a horror movie. I would rather stay in some hotel room all night, relaxing, rather than getting up at night and creeping around streets like a creepy fella, and encounter other creepy fellas, and get kidnapped by those creepy fellas… And… Just forget it. I just wanna say that I don't like this idea,' Lester said.

'Well, okay, we can *try* that, but it's not gonna be easy. I mean, there's a lot of places we'd need to search.

This is like searching your whole house for a little pencil that you misplaced.'

'But you usually find it even if you search like that, right?'

'Pretty much, yeah. That's why I said we can try it.'

'Actually, I *do* think Kevin has a point. We'd better get started on this mission, some way or the other. And I feel like this is a good one to begin with. Also, it would be a good chance for Lester to start over, and get rid of his fear of the dark, ghosts and all,' said Marrisa, chuckling at the end.

Lester looked terrified, but nodded. 'I have to do this.'

A laugh escaped from Kevin's mouth. 'You're scared of... *ghosts*?' Unable to keep it in, he burst out into an almost maniacal laughter.

'Shut up,' Marrisa said with a bossy look on her face, which actually made Kevin shut up.

'So it's settled, then. Let's use the money Mr Brown gave us. We'll have food, and a good day's sleep. Then we'll begin work, in night—I truly love gazing at the sun at dawn,' Alex said.

'And I love dusk, because it is the time to sleep,' Lester spoke rapidly, almost eating up words in between. His expression turned guarded. He muttered, 'Control, Lester. Control,' under his breath and continued, 'Forget what I said. I agree with this plan, no matter how hard it seems... To me, anyway.'

'Okay,' Alex nodded.

'Great,' Marrisa said.

'Yeah,' Kevin nodded.

'I… I guess,' said Lester.

Chapter 12

Well, we've gotten into bit of a Situation here...

They found themselves ready for the search in the evening around 7 o'clock.

'Let's do this,' Alex said as they left the hotel.

They went through alleys, dark passageways and a few big and dark farms. They didn't encounter anything special, other than a scarecrow which scared Lester and a thief, who they desperately pestered with questions after beating him up, but got nothing from. After quietly returning the stolen stuff to the owners, they sat down on a large rock near a group of trees situated next to a large warehouse on the side of a two lane road.

'This was pointless,' said Kevin, drinking from a water bottle.

'I know, man… I know,' Lester replied.

'Let's move on ahead. We're gonna go search some more. I mean, let's go look for a creepy and dark place, guys. Marrisa, don't you like horror movies?' Alex said encouragingly.

'Yeah. I do. But this is boring. Not creepy. The dark isn't what scares me. It's usually the things which lurk in it,' replied Marrisa.

'Anyway, let's move a bit more, guys. Just walk around. It'll be good exercise,' Alex said.

'I guess we should do it,' said Kevin. 'Who knows? Maybe this could be our last chance to go walking together, as *exercise*.' Kevin said curtly.

'Why am I sensing fear and pessimism in that, Kevin?' Alex said, raising an eyebrow.

'Dude, there's this big threat looming over us. We're lone travellers going around aimlessly. Why shouldn't we expect Cloedboriogd to come and slice our heads off any moment?'

'I can't do anything about your beliefs now, Kevin. Just be positive. That's all I gotta say.'

'Well, then. Let's go on, shall we?' said Kevin, standing up.

'Right,' said Alex. He took a big gulp of water from his bottle, stood up and started jogging.

The others followed him till they had gone a few miles further. Stopping for another break and a few snacks, Alex thought hard about their plan. An idea clicked him. He said, 'Remember how Mentor Vijay had taught us basic survival skills? He had taught us how to find another Sternindian using our AOPs. We could locate signs of Realm Power near us, couldn't we? I mean, maybe we can use it to locate Cloedboriogd's hideout.'

'That's GREAT!' said Lester.

'Whoa. That's something we gotta try out,' Marrisa said. 'But… Isn't it too obvious? I mean, Cloedboriogd might have thought better than making his secret base vulnerable to simple Realm Power tricks.'

'Well, whatever it is, we still gotta see if it helps. What's the harm in trying it out?' said Alex.

Alex covered his hand with a cloth, took out his AOP, swung it like a sword, successively retracting it towards his body and held it up in the air, his hand erect. He saw a red orb of light coming out of the tip of his hand-shaped AOP's index finger. Apparently, everyone else saw it too, and Lester said, 'Whoa. I couldn't have done it, man. This needs a lotta concentration.'

'I know, and I'm determined. We gotta finish this today,' replied Alex, shoving his AOP back in his pocket.

The red orb of light started floating towards Alex's friends' AOPs – which were clutched in their hands – hovering over each one for a few seconds. Then it started moving towards Alex's left, gaining speed. 'Follow it!' he shouted and started running along with the ball of light. He heard his friends' heavy footsteps behind him.

The orb made them run a pretty long distance. Alex was barely able to keep up due to exhaustion when the orb finally stopped over a large grassland, hovering mid-air. It jerked to the left, then to the right, and started floating in one direction, then moved for a few hundred meters but soon changed its path and kept moving for another few hundred meters. It stopped again, seeming confused. After a few moments, it started shaking uncontrollably, and burst into red sparks.

'Well, what does it mean?' said Lester.

'What does what mean?' Marrisa asked in reply.

'I mean, is something here? Is Cloedboriogd near? Because I don't think that that ball of light guided us anywhere. Seems like it got confused at the last second and self-destructed… kinda.'

'Yeah, I think that was it,' said Alex. 'Cloedboriogd is too smart to fall for obvious tricks.'

'Duh,' said Kevin under his breath.

'The presence of Realm Power is a bit… confusing in this area, according to what we saw the orb indicate. Just like a compass malfunctions in some areas, the indicator couldn't specifically identify the source of Realm Power here, all thanks to Cloedboriogd,' Alex said.

'Soo… Do you have any more tricks up your sleeve, Alex? Or do we all agree that we should return to Sternind and ask our principal Mr Crest to find a better person for the job? `Cause I think we ain't gonna get anywhere with these stupid basics of Realm Power. We aren't even qualified in simple stuff, so how the hell can Vishwaroopaha expect us to find a *demon*?' Kevin snapped.

'Well…' Alex shrugged, not knowing what to say.

'Alright, listen up,' said Marrisa, taking up the command, 'we gotta check everything out. Go around this area with an algorithm. Make a proper plan of all the places to be visited, and specific areas in this city to be searched. If we don't roll organized, then we don't roll.'

'Hmm,' Lester said.

'Alright, we're gonna do that. But after we investigate this place. We're getting hints of Realm Power's presence from this place, aren't we? I guess it means that some unusual disturbance – maybe Cloedboriogd's hideout – is present in this area. If we don't find anything here, we can go around searching more places in the locality,' Alex said.

'So what should we do? Just walk around here and there?' said Kevin.

Alex ignored him and said, 'Let's look for secret entrances, or maybe even places that only a demon, or something like a flying creature can go through. It could be anything from a hole in the ground to a large cave, though the latter isn't much likely to be it.'

'Well, you never know,' Lester said. 'Sometimes the most obvious things are the ones you're looking for. They're so obvious that you just ignore them and continue your search, thinking that you'll find the extraordinary, which actually doesn't exist. So let's not forget obvious villain's-lair entrances.'

'Words of wisdom and truth,' said Alex, holding up his hands, more in a joking than surrendering manner. He chuckled, making Lester smile.

They looked around for a while, and split up to cover more ground. Alex was with Lester when he got another idea. He closed his eyes, and began plotting his surroundings on a 3D grid, just like he had done to find

Snowy Supporters and classrooms in SIRP. He was able to see his surroundings, and he started scanning through them. He saw a bunch of trees, some large farms, and an unmaintained bare brick-walled shack.

'Guess it's worth checking out,' Alex said.

'What?' Lester asked, who had strayed a few meters away from Alex while searching for some clues.

'I tried scanning my surrounding using a 3D grid system which shows me things that are far away. Saw an old shack, and thought it was worth checking out. It's just a bit ahead from here. You wanna come with me?' Alex asked.

'Whoa, whoa. Slow down, dude. You mean you can see things that you can't? I know that I'm making no sense here, but you get my point. You can really see things through your *mind*?' Lester said in awe.

'Yep. Looks like Realm Power isn't as useless as I thought it would be.'

'That's so cool.'

'Yeah, so… You wanna come along?'

'Sure thing. I'm right behind ya.'

Soon, they reached the shack. It was made out of bricks that were left unpainted, and looked deserted. Alex decided to take a quick look inside. There was nothing but a few rats and an old and dusty mattress in the small hut. Its roof also threatened to collapse. He came out.

There stood a small and tattered net right next to the shack, and Alex wondered why he hadn't noticed it earlier in his 3D vision. It was hung in a vertical position, supported by two iron poles which had hooks that held its ends. It looked as if it was made for catching birds. But there was no one in sight who would make use of the net. The place was deserted. Even the shack stood in a dirty grassland, with loads of animal faeces on the ground.

'Seems kind of weird but obvious at the same time,' Alex said.

'Yeah, man… I mean, it's just a deserted old settlement. What can you expect?' Lester replied.

'Ah… Nothing much. Let's get back to work. We still gotta catch up with Marrisa and Kevin, see if they've found anything.'

'Right.'

They turned and started walking back, when Alex remembered what Lester had said a few minutes ago. "Sometimes the most obvious things are the ones you're looking for."

'Hey, Lester, I think I should review my actions sometimes. Your words of wisdom *are* really helpful,' Alex said.

'What?' Lester seemed confused at first. He then realized what Alex was referring to and said, 'Man, that was something I thought about at three in the morning because I couldn't sleep. Late night thinking is just as much burden to your life as it is to your brain. Just relax—Don't take it seriously.'

'No, no– I think I should. Just wait a minute. I'll be right back. Just need to, uh... be sure of something,' he said and went back towards the shack.

He approached the net and tried to notice something abnormal about it. He changed his perspective, wanting his imagination to guide him through this net's puzzle, if there was any puzzle. He wanted to touch the net, and get close to it, but he didn't. Something was stopping him. Not some invisible barrier or anything. His mind was urging him not to touch the net. His brain kept reminding him of absurd reasons like "It's really a breeding ground for bacteria" and prevented him from touching it.

He didn't know what inner conflict was going on inside him. Nevertheless, he gathered all his willpower and touched the net. The net, as it seemed, was not a piece of mesh cloth hanging from two erect iron poles, rather it was an iron structure itself. It was so deceiving that when Alex looked at it, it seemed like a real net. But when he touched it, he knew that there was something strange about it.

He came to think about all the reasons Cloedboriogd's hideout's entrance could be this net. It was disguised as a realistic looking net for catching birds, in a dirty and deserted place and in the area where Realm Power went a bit haywire. It was also protected by some kind of charm that prompted the guy who was curious enough to approach it, to not touch it.

'Cloedboriogd is smart, knowing that flying creatures avoid nets, and this one's certainly not big enough to fit a whole person inside it, much less a demon like

Cloedboriogd who has wings. It would certainly throw almost anyone off the trail. If it weren't for Lester's advice, I wouldn't have gotten this far,' Alex thought, a smile coming over his face. This was the second time Lester had helped him in a difficult situation. The first advice he had given to him was "Right is always right", and that had kind of helped him out.

Alex called out to Lester in a loud voice, 'Hey, dude, over here!'

'What's it?' Lester asked curiously.

Alex explained what he had just found and its significance. Lester's eyes widened as soon as Alex stopped speaking. 'I'll be back with Marrisa and Kevin,' he said and ran back in the opposite direction.

'Wait a minute, I just need to be sure,' Alex thought to himself. 'Gotta throw something inside, to know whether it's actually a portal to some other place or not.'

An idea was starting to form in his mind. He recalled a technique that was taught to him in SIRP. Mentor Chakravarti had explained, 'Along with your Supporters, you can also ask any animal for help, if you are in a situation that requires you to have an experimental asset for your needs. The animals just need enough Realm Power, which is a healing substance for their soul, which they receive from you in return for the help you get by them. And the source for that Realm Power has to be your AOP. You can control any animal this way, though it works only for a few minutes, or as long as the animal's need for Realm Power is fulfilled. For example, a bird is a small animal, so you can only control it for five to ten minutes. Whereas, an elephant is a larger animal, and even though it might be hard to establish such a connection with it in the first place, you can control it for twelve hours.'

He remembered his lesson on controlling a bird.

'You must hold your AOP in a horizontal position, and visually line it with any of the birds flying in the sky, according to your field of vision and sight. Then you must start mimicking the bird's motions with your AOP for a few moments, and after seeing if it starts reacting to the Realm Power you send its way. You must judge the connection you have formed with it according to its reactions to the process.

Case I - If the bird starts looking paranoid, you must stop the process of trying to get its attention immediately, or you'll… Let's just say, overload it with Realm Power, causing it to die. This is because the bird has not accepted your connection with it, and is continuously denying your invitation, but if you keep on troubling it by providing it excess Realm Power, it will eventually not be able to withstand it and could be knocked unconscious or worse, die.

Case II - If the bird starts accepting Realm Power from your AOP, you can be the source of its next movements. In that case, the bird will start mimicking your AOP's actions if it has accepted the request for help sent by your AOP. So, you can use your AOP as a mode to control the bird, thus sharing a mutual understanding of Realm Power in exchange for temporary control over the bird's body.'

Alex tried this technique a few times with his AOP, but failed. Maybe physical contact with his AOP was required for it. Maybe he just couldn't do it because he had a cloth separating his skin from the surface of his Primo, all thanks to Cloedboriogd. He almost wanted to *shout* curses at him, then and there, not caring whether he was near the supposed entrance of his hideout. He absolutely loathed Cloedboriogd as he recalled how that demon had ruined Angelina's life, and how he was now trying to get to Alex by using his own Primo against him.

Suddenly, he noticed Marrisa, Kevin and Lester coming back, running and panting. 'Is it true?' Marrisa asked immediately as she reached within audible distance.

'Well, yeah. Or so it seems,' Alex replied. Then he explained to them in depth about what he was thinking of doing. He told them that he was thinking of trying to control a bird, and guide it through a small gap in the net. 'We'll see if it disappears into one of the comparatively bigger holes. That'll indicate the entrance to some invisible portal to Cloedboriogd's hideout,' Alex finished.

'So… Did you do it?' asked Kevin.

'If I did, I won't be explaining this shit to you right now,' Alex replied.

'Leave that to me,' Marrisa said. She pulled out her AOP, which was shaped like a stick with artistic and intricate carvings on it. She successfully controlled a pigeon in her first try, and guided it into the net. It disappeared with a pop sound.

'Guess that confirms it,' Marrisa said. 'Good job, Alex.'

'Whoa. You really *are* good at all this,' Alex said.

'Oh, you don't really know what all I'm good at, honey,' Marrisa said, winking at Alex. She chuckled a few seconds later after seeing his blank expression.

'Um, what was that?' said Kevin, rapidly darting his eyes between Alex and Marrisa.

'What do you think?' said Marrisa, raising an eyebrow.

'Well– Uhm, were you f–'

'It doesn't matter, Kevin, okay? You shouldn't pay heed to such little things. It's above your level of understanding—Or more precisely, *common sense*,' Marrisa replied, giving her brother a sheepish look.

'Got a bit too awkward there,' Lester said in a hushed but high pitched voice.

Not knowing what to think about it all, Alex said, 'Yeah, so… Let's get right back on track. I was thinking, now that we're sure that this is the place, we gotta find a way to get in. This net looks a bit weird, considering it's made of something as hard as iron. We can't possibly go through it, unless we can get as small as that bird we just sent in.'

'Yeah… But before we try to find a way to go through, how can we be so sure that we're gonna end up in Cloedboriogd's hideout? What if it's a trap set by him, with large metal spikes waiting for us at the end of a long fall as soon as we get in? What if we're dealing with some other monster? What if…' Kevin said apprehensively.

'Guess one of us will have to go in, make sure that we're going to the right place. Then he'll call out to the others, telling them it's safe to come in,' Lester said.

'But what if there's no way of getting sound through the portal? And how do we know that the bird didn't just disintegrate?' Kevin said.

'So you think we're just gonna have one guy do all the *sacrifices*, then? If it comes down to the worst, we're all dying together, okay? We're going to go through the portal together, and we'll survive. We gotta trust ourselves on that. And Kevin, you really need to stop being such an apprehensive nerd who always starts jumping to negative conclusions,' Alex snapped.

'Alright, dude, alright. Slow down,' Kevin said in a guarded tone.

'Now let's find a way to go in through that small hole, shall we?' Lester said.

'Yeah… I'm thinking of looking around a bit more, trying to find something,' Alex said.

He then went back into the shack, without waiting for a response from anyone. Looking around carefully, he noticed how the walls had some patches of dirt swept off of them. It was as if some large cloth had whipped around in the shack, displacing a bit of dirt and rubble.

'Wings,' Alex thought. 'Of Cloedboriogd. There should be something in here that's needed to activate something in the net, maybe make it large enough for someone as big as a demon to go through.'

He investigated further, hoping to find some switch or lever, which usually does mechanical jobs like opening a machine-operated door, or in this case, enlarging a net.

He finally found it. It was a piece of rusty metal jutting out from a crack in a wall. It was just like a lever, pulled down. Maybe if Alex pulled it up…

As soon as he did it, he heard one of his friends shout, 'Something's happening!'

He ran back out, and saw the net becoming bigger, slowly mending itself, and transforming into a cylindrical shape as it hovered in the air, free from the iron poles that it was apparently hung on. His friends were right there, looking at the net as if it were some mythical creature that they all admired. Alex remained cautious while analyzing the situation.

But before he could even think of doing anything, the net transformed into a strong metal cage and dropped itself on top of Alex and his friends, trapping them. And that's when everything went black.

Everything outside the cage vanished, as if wiped out of existence. Alex heard a loud whirring sound, like the cage was traveling somewhere using jet engine turbines. His friends looked panicked and were yelling among the chaos. He screamed, 'Calm down! We're getting close! Remember what we had discussed—Choose your words carefully!'

Something came over all of his friends, and they appeared confident, with guarded expressions on their faces. It seemed like they knew what was coming and were prepared for it. Alex was prepared too. Or so he thought. He honestly didn't know how they were going to pull this off.

The view cleared, and Alex found him and his friends in a dark underground hallway, the cage dissolving into thin air. There wasn't much illumination, just a few dim torches placed at large but regular intervals on the stone walls. Even though the place was pretty dark, Alex could see some large claw marks and blood splotches on the walls.

'I like it dark, you know,' someone said. Alex immediately recognized Cloedboriogd's voice, it was the same voice Angelina had spoken in—First at Wasor and then in SIRP. Speaking of Angelina… Alex half expected for her to show up right next to Cloedboriogd, or worse… *as* Cloedboriogd.

The demon's voice bounced off the walls in a deep echo. Alex immediately grabbed a torch from the wall. Lester's eyes widened. Kevin didn't seem like he could even stand.

'Well, well, well. Looks like I've got some visitors,' Cloedboriogd continued. He was nowhere to be seen in the darkness. 'So give me a reason why I shouldn't rip you to shreds for trespassing. You are such dumb kids. What was the need of poking around only to meet your death? I am so deeply grieved at the loss of your lives, but seems like you need to die. Maybe I'll just use one of your

Articles Of Power to send a message to SIRP, especially to their principal who sent you here to find me.'

Alex was shocked. How did Cloedboriogd know?

'Who are you? You're a Sternindian too?' Marrisa shouted in a shaky voice, trying to imply that she didn't know who Cloedboriogd was.

The demon appeared out of the shadows, and it was a sight Alex could never forget. Cloedboriogd was nothing like what he had expected. At first glance, he looked quite skinny, not really muscular or hairy. Instead, he was a black-skinned monster, with long pointed talons and large wings, sharp eyes and a really big mouth. His legs seemed like they could snap any moment, but his expression showed signs of pure malice. The weirdest thing was that each time Alex looked at him, his vision spun, and he could see different forms of his body—Once with flames burning all over his body, another with his head shaped like a skull, and even one in which he was looking as if he spent his whole life in the gym.

It was quite shocking, terrifying and intriguing at the same time. 'Oh, you don't know, huh?' Cloedboriogd said, coming closer towards them. He turned towards Marrisa, and touched her chin with his talon, causing a drop of blood to trickle down her neck. To Alex's surprise, she didn't flinch.

Within a second, Cloedboriogd grabbed her by the neck and threw her a few feet away, her body slamming into the wall. 'No!' Kevin shouted. The torch fell from Alex's hand.

'Please, stop. It's not what it seems like,' Alex spoke up, to distract Cloedboriogd. 'I'm Alex, and these are my friends. We are from Sternind, and it's true that we came here intentionally, but it was all due to curiosity,' Alex started, realizing halfway how bad this was going. 'We were chosen to be in Sternind, but we... D- Didn't like it there. W- We were afraid of everything there. We wanted to escape and go back to Earth. So we found a portal that opened up in India, and we decided to find a way back to our home. We were looking for signs of any Realm Power operated transportation device, and that's how we found your… Place. I- I'm just speaking up because it isn't what it seems like, and you're p- probably going to kill us anyway, so…' Alex fell to his knees and started sobbing, which was partly fake, and partly real, since he *was* scared, after all.

'You're talking extemporarily. A little bit of stammer, hmm… Maybe you're telling the truth. I think I'll keep you here for a while, have fun with you,' said Cloedboriogd as he stared into Alex's red eyes, smiling. Alex broke eye contact to keep up the pretence.

Kevin kneeled down next to Alex and hung his head. Lester ran to Marrisa. 'So, let's see how you all can make yourselves useful. Well, I mostly make deals with people, and one of those stupid guys even took me… Wait a second, I've got it—We've got something to do! Let's start with a story, shall we?' Cloedboriogd said slowly, stressing the word *story*.

Alex was preparing himself for saying "Yes" in the most

whimper-like way he could imagine, but Cloedboriogd didn't wait for him.

'So,' the demon said, 'this just came to my mind when I was talking about deals. You see, I'm a Majenimal who only believes in actions. But I like deals, too. Especially the ones with blood involved. You know, you mortals make deals with others to avoid conflicts, right? As for me, I don't care about the deal, but I do like to add conflicts *within* the deal. And that's what this story is based on. You see, I was dealing with this guy called Noah Parkinson, and he was totally prepared for it! Like, can you believe that? He already knew about me, and, well, those were the glorious times, so I was famous…'

But, anyway, Noah asked for a part of *me* in return for his family, wealth, and his heart. I liked devouring their souls, but what I did not like was my part of the bargain. That stupid piece of shit literally trapped a small part of my soul in a bottle! I still like to imagine what I'd do to him if he was if front of me, even though I know he's dead. But why did he want to split my soul? To make me weaker? I do not know. The thing is that I do not know where that part of my soul is, where he's hidden it. And what's astonishing is that I do not even know whether it's released from the bottle yet! I can't even feel myself! I feel inferior comparing myself to a genie! Such agony, and there was no one to share my thoughts with. So I decided to tell you this interesting story. Did you like it?'

'Y- Yes,' said Kevin.

'So... Uh… Um- Are we free to go?' Lester said from behind Cloedboriogd, helping Marrisa up. She staggered but righted herself.

'I guess you are, but the question is, *how* will you go? How will you escape my humble home until I show you the way?' Cloedboriogd said, smiling.

'Oh, crap,' Kevin muttered.

Cloedboriogd spoke abruptly as he turned back and gestured with his hand. 'Follow me, kiddos. I've got something to show you. Let's have a little chat, and then I'll decide whether you all will go back with or without your limbs.'

Chapter 13

This was not supposed to happen, was it?

Cloedboriogd led them through the same underground tunnel-like pathway, taking occasional turns at a few diversions. Alex made note of every turn and tried to learn it, in case they had to escape back through the same route. The narrow tunnel opened into a large area, which looked like a large hangar, capable of storing two to three private jets. The place was totally trashed, with rubble littering the floor, flickering lights dangling from the ceiling, and various things like oil, machine parts scattered here and there. Alex even noticed a half-melted plane engine sitting in a corner of the room, as if to say **You see me? I'm melted and discarded. You're gonna be like me too, once Cloedboriogd gets his job done using you.**

'I haven't had guests for quite a while, you know. And the ones I've had aren't as smart as you. I think I'll be friends with you for a while before I get a chance to taste your souls. So, I–'

'What's the deal?' Kevin said in a loud voice, cutting Cloedboriogd off. 'Stop the nonsense. I know you're a demon and you're gonna kill us eventually, but let's not overdo this, okay? We don't wanna be friends with you, so just get straight to the point.'

'Considering this outrageous show of rudeness, I swear if you weren't of great use to me, I would've picked up your body and turned it into grey slop right this instant– I call it Soul Porridge. But you're right, I guess. I want you all to get something for me,' Cloedboriogd replied calmly.

'What is it?' Alex asked, looking straight up at Cloedboriogd, trying to fight his unstable vision.

'Oh, it's nothing. I just want you all to go and get me a small and useless Article Of Power shaped like a hand. But be prepared for death,' Cloedboriogd said.

Alex tried to understand. An Article Of Power shaped like a hand was none other than one of the Primos. Cloedboriogd might be asking for the second Primo to be brought back to him, maybe because the Sternindians might've put some restrictions on it as a safety measure if Cloedboriogd attempted to escape from the prison. But if the AOP was right next to Cloedboriogd, then what prevented him from using Realm Power on the AOP to be able to get rid of the restriction and use it?

'No, no. This can't be true. Cloedboriogd has the AOP for sure. Otherwise how could he try to manipulate my Primo using his, if he doesn't even have it in the first place? Maybe he's trying to trap us. Whatever it is, I'm gonna check it out myself. There's no need to drag my friends into this. I think me and Alexander will have to do the job alone. Marrisa needs care, and Kevin and Lester can handle the situation for a few moments while I'm gone. I know how to do this,' Alex thought.

'I'll go. Alone,' he said. 'But you have to set my friends free in return.'

'No, Alex. That isn't quite the deal I offer. Is there any cutting of limbs or eating of souls involved? No. Is there any loss of money or any blood involved? No. Yeah, you could die on the way, but still… I can't agree to this.'

'Okay– Keep them here. Make them hostages and use them as your insurance or whatever, I don't care. At least they'll be safer here with you than with what's out there that even a Majenimal like you can't defeat,' Alex said, trying to be brave.

'You're pretty attentive, Alex. You kept it in mind when I said that I was a Majenimal. You can be of use to me, but first you need to prove yourself…' Cloedboriogd said.

Alex already knew that Cloedboriogd was a Majenimal, but it seemed like the demon did not have a hint of it. Cloedboriogd must be thinking that Alex had just got to know about him. This assured Alex that Cloedboriogd really knew little about them, and was just lying to try and get more information.

'I've had enough of proving, okay?' Alex said in a loud

voice. 'Now I'm gonna go, and I'm hoping you won't… take any harsh decisions.'

'Oh, don't worry,' Cloedboriogd said with a malicious smile, looking at Lester, Marrisa and Kevin. 'They'll be taken care of.'

Alex's eyes widened.

'I mean I'll take care of them,' Cloedboriogd said with a confused expression on his face. 'Did I say anything wrong? I haven't quite spoken English for a while.'

'No. Nothing. Just leave it,' Alex said as he looked around, trying not to worry much about his friends. He knew he was, in a way, running away when his friends were in danger but he also knew he had no other choice. 'Where do I have to go?' he said.

'Oh, just follow the blood.'

He noticed no splotches, but large puddles and splash marks of a red liquid on the ground—the blood Cloedboriogd was referring to. Alex was surprised he hadn't noticed this earlier.

'Don't worry, Alex. This blood belongs – or should I say *belonged* – to some Indian guests who stumbled upon my magnificent home an hour ago. They were unworthy to have an audience with me, so I sent them straight to hell,' Cloedboriogd said.

Alex said nothing as he turned towards the blood and started following the trail. This was surely the blood of someone Cloedboriogd had dragged across the ground and taken to some place he'd killed them later. Now, he was trying to lead Alex straight towards it.

Alex patted his pockets to make sure his CY device was with him, and jogged with it until the trail of blood led him into yet another tunnel, away from the hangar-like room the rest were in. There was barely any illumination, which made him even more scared than the recent events. He was on edge.

As soon as he was sure that he was out of Cloedboriogd's sight, he brought out his CY device, switched it on and started using its light to see through the darkness. 'Hoi!' Alexander said in a loud voice.

'Shh,' Alex said.

'Wait, where are we going?'

'You know we had to sabotage Cloedboriogd's security systems, right? I've managed to get away from him and now we're underground, in this network of tunnels. I don't know where we're going, but–'

'WATCH OUT!'

Alex moved aside with lightning speed as a snake jumped out of the darkness, right in front of his face. His CY device fell from his hand, its light illuminating the floor. He saw the large hideous Cobra, venom dripping from its mouth. Its scaly body was covered with colourful patterns.

'Alright, I'm outta here,' Alex thought as he quickly scooped up his CY device and continued running further into the tunnel. There was no turning back now.

'The element of surprise, huh?' Alexander said. 'Glad you escaped, boss.'

He ran for what seemed like centuries, not stopping

for even a second, even though it felt like his heart would burst through his chest any moment. A few moments later, he noticed that the ground was getting slippery.

He shone light upon the floor. Whatever it was splattered with blood—Lots of it.

'I've always imagined what a torture chamber would be like. Now I think I've seen one,' Alexander said.

'It's worse. Seems like Cloedboriogd has sent me into a place where he's set up some kind of mechanism to kill anyone that comes though.'

'Yeah. And we're not gonna get out of this, unless…'

'Unless?'

'Unless we find out the right way. This seems like a labyrinth, but there's no clear plan or goal of what to follow or where to go. There is barely any light, so we can expect to find tunnels branching out from here which are designed to not be noticeable. And from what I know, villains keep their secrets in either the most secure of places, or the most insecure and dangerous of places. I've seen Cloedboriogd, and I personally think he's a psycho, so I guess he can be called insecure *and* dangerous,' Alexander said.

'Insecure and dangerous. Yeah. I totally agree,' Alex said mid-gasp.

'Looks like Sternindian AI has gotten really far,' he thought afterwards as he considered what Alexander had said.

'No, no, no, no, no…' Alexander kept muttering.

'What?' Alex said, irritated.

'We're running straight into a trap. You know it, and I know it. There's no security systems here. Nothing other than death. THEN WHY THE HECK ARE YOU RUNNING FURTHER?'

The rush of Adrenalin had almost made Alex mad, and all the while it took him a moment to realize that he'd probably also lost his common sense. He figured it'd be better to run back and take his chances with Cloedboriogd. He stopped, and stood in the darkness for a while, being able to hear his breath as if a storm were blowing inside him.

He regained his senses, and felt the blood rushing to his brain. Shaking convulsively, he gathered the last bit of willpower to turn back and jog in the direction which he came from. But before he could move a step, the ground rumbled.

Rubble started falling from above, and the ground beneath him transformed, sloping downwards. He lost his grip and slid down; screaming and trying to grab onto any hand hold he could find. The ground and roof turned almost vertical, and Alex found himself in the air, away from the surfaces of the dark tunnel, falling at a greater speed. His CY device fell from his hand, and was lost in the chaos.

Something hit his head – a large hard rock – and he was knocked unconscious—Yet again.

Thanks to his consciousness's defiant nature, he woke up, and to his amazement, he had sustained heavy damage to his head. The right side of his head throbbed badly, and before he even opened his eyes, he could feel the blood dripping down his face, and onto his neck.

His right eye refused to function properly, but unfazed, he forcibly opened both of his eyes, and got up to look around.

He was in a small and dark room, and couldn't see anything but moonlight peeping from an opening in the roof. Only one thing could prevent him from rotting here forever. He decided to forget thinking about other escape routes and rely on the one and only—Realm Power.

He scanned everything around him, and found that he was just above the hangar-like room, where Cloedboriogd was with his friends. He could even detect their red-coloured heat signatures in his Realm Power 3-D grid.

Alex was surprised that the ground could hold his weight considering it was thin and only made up of loose and wet soil. He dug down furiously, and successfully managed to make a fist-sized hole in the ground. He started widening the hole, until it was big enough to fit him in. Nothing could stop him now. He figured he was half dead already, so even if it were a big jump down there, he'd survive it. His instincts told him that. Or maybe it was just Realm Power.

He remembered Alexander. But there was no use searching for him now. Alex needed medical help, and

Alexander wasn't even a real person. 'Do I want to save an AI? Maybe… Maybe not. I'll come for him later. Or will I?' Alex thought, feeling disturbed. This chain of thoughts was pointless in the situation.

He jumped through the hole, and landed on his feet, twisting his ankle. He feel onto the ground, groaning with uncontrollable pain.

'Not Sternindians uninterested in Realm Power, are we, Alex?' Cloedboriogd said as he leaned over Alex. 'I just wanted to see if you'd fall for the trap or you'd prove that the story you told us is made-up. You couldn't have gotten out of that room without using Realm Power, and seems like you knew just how to make use of it to escape. I think you should've done your homework before coming to face me.'

Cloedboriogd grabbed Alex by his neck and set him down with his back against one of the walls. 'Sit tight, and enjoy the view,' Cloedboriogd said, gesturing towards Alex's friends.

Right next to the half-melted plane engine, was a large glass capsule used as a cage, with Lester in it, who looked like he had been beaten mercilessly. Marrisa lay a few feet away, with a knife in her stomach, her blood-stained hand clutching its handle. Her eyes were wide with shock. Kevin was just next to her, knocked out on the floor.

'You see, your friends here have been taken care of, just as I promised,' Cloedboriogd said, gesturing towards Alex's friends, looking pleased with himself. 'I know right about everything now. Well, what I knew of you earlier, Alex, was that someone with a group of friends knows about me, and is trying to act upon some kind of a plan. And it came as a surprise that those kids were you. Seriously, your principal was quite a smart man, sending kids to do their job, so that I won't get suspicious. When I said that that Article of Power is small and useless, why didn't you question its importance? When I said that that blood was of some other victims of mine, why weren't you curious about how I killed a bunch of innocent people just because of their *unworthiness*? You're clever, but not clever enough to challenge me. You knew it was a trap, but, you see, traps are one of the things I'm an expert at setting. You tried to go alone for this fake deal I offered you, but what I gathered from you is that you keep your friends' lives above yours most of the time. I wanted to separate you from them so I could test the truth in your story. Well, now you see what you've gotten yourself into.'

After a short pause, Cloedboriogd continued, 'Plus, your friends here won't just stop acting, pretending like they knew nothing. So I had to do something for them,' he paused as he gave a devilish smile and then continued, 'You're nice, helpful, and a man of principles, Alex. But you can't always expect the so-called *fair, just and right* side of the war to win, can you? What you see here, Alex, is the reason the Savage Person and I ruled in that glorious era. We are naturally smarter and better.'

'Tell me his name,' Alex said, feeling half-dead from inside.

'I'm sorry, what?' Cloedboriogd replied, apparently trying to be polite after all he had done to Alex's friends.

'I SAID TELL ME HIS NAME! WHY DO YOU CALL HIM THE SAVAGE PERSON, HUH? You are his Supporter. Y-You know him. Then why…?' Alex could not complete his sentence. His heavy breaths overshadowed his voice. He wanted to know everything before he breathed his final breath in. Dying ignorant was not how Alex wanted to die.

'Alas, that is not for you to know,' Cloedboriogd said, as he stretched his hand out towards Alex. Alex felt a disturbance in Realm Power quickly grab hold of him, as if a large hand was enclosing him in its grip. Cloedboriogd controlled the hand as he rose Alex up in the air and threw him into a small room in one corner of the hangar that looked like any ordinary prison cell on Earth. This room was totally different from the modern environment of the place like the Hangar.

Alex was frustrated and suffering. He really wanted to end all this right then, no matter how he did it. This was one of the moments when he had finally lost hope. He really couldn't take it anymore.

'FINE, THEN!' Alex shouted as loudly as he could. 'DO WHATEVER YOU WANNA DO! KILL US! GO AHEAD! TAKE THE PRIMO!'

'See, that's exactly what you don't understand about me, Alex,' Cloedboriogd said, staring deep into Alex's eyes, making him dizzy. 'And that's another reason you couldn't trick—much less defeat me. The thing is, I can have many personalities. I'd like to say, that I'm… Unpredictable.'

'What do you want, then?' Alex said, feeling weaker than ever.

'You know, I don't like getting things the easy way. In life, you have to work hard to accomplish your main goal. And that has kind of become my habit now,' Cloedboriogd replied, chuckling in all his malice and demonic glory.

Alex didn't say anything. He just focused on not breaking eye contact.

After a few moments of painful silence, Cloedboriogd spoke up, 'So here's the thing – Fair and square, neat and clear – I'm going to accept the Primo you currently have in your pocket only if you give it to me. I really want it to escape from Earth, but come to think of it… What's the hurry? Considering that I've already managed to fail your little "plan", I think I've got nothing to lose.'

Alex grasped that Cloedboriogd was evil, but not wrong. He was teasing him, and there was nothing he could do about it.

Now Alex truly felt all the pressure on him. His friends relied on him. Earth relied on him. Heck, the three realms relied on him. But there was no choice. If death was his fate, so be it. He decided to give Cloedboriogd his Primo, the second AOP that the demon would need to escape Earth, meet The Savage Person and bring the old misery back to the three realms once and for all.

While Alex was thinking, Cloedboriogd looked as

if concentrating on Lester in the glass cage. He moved his fingers quickly and furiously to use Realm Power and… 'Oh god,' Alex thought, horrified, as he saw what Cloedboriogdhad done.

Cloedboriogd started laughing mercilessly as he pulled Lester's body apart, forming deep wounds at his joints, which slowly lined with blood, successively soaking his clothes and staining them red. His screams were silent, though. Alex figured that he was imprisoned in a glass cage for a reason. It was soundproof.

Lester's face contorted as he struggled to try and keep his body together, flailing. Alex stared at Lester, shocked and grieved, as his hands, limbs, torso, and head all came apart. The blood was seemingly immeasurable, spreading everywhere. Alex couldn't hold it anymore. He burst out crying.

'PLEASE, STOP!' he shouted.

'Oh, yeah?' Cloedboriogd said as he joined Lester's body back, filling all the lost blood back inside him, mending his muscles and nerves—Bringing him back to life. 'Well, I knew that would get you going. Now, hand over the AOP.'

Alex was terrified.

'Yeah, I will. But before that,' Alex asked, astonished, 'So this wasn't… real? Lester d-didn't suffer? It was a-all a h-hologram?' He sobbed while speaking, his voice cracking.

'Oh no, dear, it wasn't an illusion. See,' Cloedboriogd said annoyingly, and repeated the process. He tore Lester apart to small body parts, and then to shreds. A few moments later, after lots of blood, he was re-joined.

Cloedboriogd calling Alex "dear" added to the fast deterioration of his mental health. He was done—For real this time. He averted his eyes at the sight of Cloedboriogd and drifted away from him, trying to get lost in his own thoughts. He closed his eyes and rested his head on the wall, wounded, disregarded, disrespected and hopeless. A tear trickled down his cheek as it mixed with his blood, and moved down his neck only to stop with no effect.

Alex could not believe what he had seen a few moments before. Such brutality seemed unreal. He felt... Broken from inside, as he had never felt before. Ever. All his courage felt as if it had... Gone.

Suddenly, his ears started ringing, the pressure inside them increasing. He perked up and looked around. It took him a few moments to realize that everything had... Stopped. Cloedboriogd wasn't moving. Neither were his friends. He couldn't even feel his heartbeat. It felt quite a bit like the time Vishwaroopaha had paused everything, only much, *much* more powerful.

Time had stopped.

Surprised, Alex looked around, trying to find the cause of this strangeness. But before he could even move his head, a ghoul appeared in front of him, transiting through the wall. It was a hooded figure the size of an average human, looking much like the depiction of death itself. The only difference was that it had a book in its hand rather than a scythe.

It said in a cracking voice–

When destiny does not change its tracks,
But you need that the most
For when death is near,
But you don't dread it at all costs

The Lost Cabin finds a way
To help a warrior
Who is never scared of painful failure

But remember
The Lost Cabin appears in exchange of a price which involves pain

Which, if not made to bear
In your case,
Would lead to the rise of the one who instills most fear

The most likely thing to happen
Next you have to utter
And what you need most of The Lost Cabin shall show up–
The Entrance Shutter.

Chapter 14

The Lost Cabin

'A ghoul reciting a poem. This has crossed all limits of weirdness,' Alex thought, trying to take it lightly. A fire of hope kindled within him, along with the scent of suspicion. 'As if I haven't already had enough of entrance shutters back at Wasor,' he thought. 'Well, seems like this is the only way to go. What is this thing, anyway?'

He recalled something about a place named "The Lost Cabin". When he was in Realm Geo class, a kid had asked a random question, not related to Realm Geo. Rather, it seemed related to history. He sure did involve the words "The Lost Cabin" in his question.

Mentor Smith had said, 'The Lost Cabin is a place which is only *rumoured* to exist. It is said that it's a room-like closed structure, where the lord of Creation Om, had created a very important aspect of our lives—Fate. He had also created several other things which were so large in number that even he himself, the supreme lord couldn't keep track of them. He soon found out that he had lost the whereabouts of his Cabin among his other creations. It was where he had created the very destiny of everyone, including his own. He decided to give up on finding it, and hoped that it was better lost, for no one could misuse it. And so it was named—The Lost Cabin. More random facts about this rumour are that The Lost Cabin had developed its own mind, by intermingling with other spheres of lord Om's creations. It had the essence of Fate's power, the creative mind of lord Om, the sneaky and twisted qualities of a stealthy veil, which The Lost Cabin used to conceal itself from the world, and someday, as it thought, to reveal itself in order to be of use to the one in Millions. It became a place that allowed people to… um… Alter their course of life. You can say that it could help someone change destiny of anyone. But… You know it's just a rumour, so you better take it as one. Now focus on the lesson, and no out-of-the-box questions!'

'Oh my god. This can't be happening…' Alex thought. He was as excited as much he was scared. He pondered over the words the ghoul said. A few seconds passed by, with the ghoul floating in the air in front of Alex. Oh wait. Actually, time didn't pass by. It was stopped. Everything was still, except for Alex and the ghoul.

'Let's forget everything else, but just focus on getting into The Lost Cabin. Seems like I need to solve some kind of puzzle by uttering "the most likely thing to happen next",' Alex figured. Or that was what he *thought*. He wasn't sure that was exactly what he had do.

It seemed too difficult, or too easy. "The most likely thing to happen next", as in when? The thing that would happen after Alex gives Cloedboriogd the AOP? The thing that would happen after Cloedboriogd finds the part of his soul imprisoned in a bottle? The thing that would happen with Alex after the ghoul recited some kind of a poem in front of him?

Whatever it was, Alex immediately understood he was really bad at predictions. Also, the word "thing" didn't quite specify the situation. Alex was confused out of his wits.

He couldn't think much about it. He finally settled on a simple conclusion. To think positive. He decided to say – or utter – the thing that was most likely to happen if Alex and his friends had succeeded in their plan. This seemed like the least expected answer, and that is why Alex went along with it.

He said to the mysterious ghoul, 'After me and my friends succeed in sabotaging the demon's security systems, we'll watch as Alexander gives allies the signal. SIRP's principal will come with his reinforcements to securely imprison Cloedboriogd forever, and prevent a huge disaster from taking place.'

This was what Alex wanted. But what he said was just to gain entry into The Lost Cabin. Reality couldn't be whatever he wanted it to be. Not this easily.

This seemed like yet another test, to prove that he was the right person to have access to The Lost Cabin. He was not met with disappointment when the ghoul replied, 'You have a clear and positive goal in mind. Positivity is what drives fate, even if the outcomes are not always positive. You are hereby qualified for the entry into The Lost Cabin.'

Alex braced himself, trying not to let joy take over, even though it wasn't so likely. Suddenly, the bricks of the wall started breaking and smashing against each other, crumbling to dust. A few moments later, a door-sized opening in the prison wall was before Alex.

Alex knew what had to be done. Starting to regain courage, he got up on his feet, shaking, and went through the wall.

As soon as he entered, he was greeted with two shining screens in a pitch-black room. Both the screens resembled projection screens of movie theatres; large rectangular boxes displaying *figures* in a loop, or if more appropriately put, *scenes*.

This reminded Alex of the hologram maze at Wasor, which had played with everyone's minds using scenes or holograms, confusing them to prevent them from finding the right path. But that was different.

These two scenes were being shown adjacent to each other. Alex figured that he had to choose one of these. He was limited to two fates.

The first scene showed Cloedboriogd closing in on Alex's friends, who were badly wounded and running from the demon in a forest. Just as the demon approached them and was about to kill them, Alex appeared behind him and used his AOP to beat Cloedboriogd. The scene ended right there, no consequences defined.

He was amazed. Was this actually possible?

Not deciding to delve into the fake world of temptations, he decided to view the second scene before making his choice.

The second scene showed Alex with both the Primos in his hands, they flew from Cloedboriogd's grip and landed into his arms. His eyes glowed green, and he shouted as he charged—The scene ended.

'Nothing's specified. In the first scene, even if I beat Cloedboriogd, what prevents him from stealing my AOP and using both of them to escape from Earth? In the second scene, where are my friends? Are they safe? Or are they suffering? Maybe even near death, like they are right now…? What would I even do if I get both the AOPs? Will I fight him and try to get to my friends? But then how will I possibly escape?' Alex thought.

He started having an emotional breakdown. Now he had to choose between saving the Realms or saving his friends?

"The world is a cruel place, Alex" he remembered his father teaching him. "So make your decisions wisely."

Vishwaroopaha had also said, "Surroundings are going to be deceptive".

Something changed inside Alex—It was a feeling of… Mysterious but dreadful *happiness*. He did not know what he was feeling, but he decided to go with what *he* felt was right, and not be deceived by the scenes. He shouted, 'I choose the second choice,' hoping for The Lost Cabin to understand.

Alex watched as everything around him dissolved into nothingness bit by bit. He was ready to fight Cloedboriogd, if that meant he would get to use both the AOPs in his fight. The rest would be thought about later on, *if* he won.

A few moments later, he found himself standing in the prison cell, with both the AOPs in his hands. He readied himself for the "epic" fight that was about to happen, or that was what his subconscious brain termed it as.

But within a second, the world dissolved again, and he found himself lying in his bunk in his Dorm at SIRP, completely healed.

WHAT HAD HAPPENED?

Chapter 15

Revelations

Alex got down from his bunk and checked his pockets and hands. He had no AOP with him. What was happening?

He found Lester a few feet away, screaming at the sight of him as a large smile spread across his face. He was also looking fine, with not a single dirt patch on his clothes.

'Dude! What's happening?' Alex asked him.

'I have no idea,' Lester replied. 'One moment I'm being tortured in a glass cage, the next I'm here.'

'Okay… I've got a lot to say, and a *lot more* to ask, so…'

'Wait. Let me get the others.'

To Alex's amazement, a few minutes later Lester, Kevin, Marrisa, Vishwaroopaha and even Angelina had gathered in the boys' Dorm. Angelina? How was she here?

Alex told them his story, eating up words in between excitedly, and quickly finished speaking.

Vishwaroopaha replied, 'Now you might be thinking how the somewhat opposite of what you had chosen followed. I am in a thoughtful trance, too. But what I have drawn from this is that you surely had the AOPs delivered in your hands– both of them, when you were in your prison cell. The AOPs had flied to you miraculously, but before you could realize it, you yourself had disappeared the very next second from that prison.'

'Oh. But what about…' Alex said in bewilderment, gesturing towards his friends. 'Them? And Angelina? How are *you* here? You were possessed! By Cloedboriogd!' He could not understand anything.

'Sit down, boy,' Vishwaroopaha said as he gestured towards Alex's bunk. 'Before I explain anything, I want you to be calm. Also, I would like to clear that this was not planned by me, and was the reality. So don't be under the impression that this was also like Wasor Island.'

'Right,' Alex said as he sat down.

Vishwaroopaha started, 'When you disappeared, your friends fainted. They told me that all of them, in their minds, felt like they were dying, but in reality, they weren't. They later woke up in the same place where they were earlier, only Cloedboriogd's hideout and everything was gone. They met Angelina right there. Seems like Cloedboriogd doesn't need her anymore. We have some idea why he did so.'

'Wha–' instead of giving a remark, Alex decided he

wanted to know further. 'What is it?'

'Remember the story Cloedboriogd told you at his hideout, in which he stated that a small part of his soul was split apart, and trapped in a bottle? Maybe that part of his soul was the one controlling Angelina, not the one you met in India. He has, for some reason, set Angelina free from his grasp. We think that the part of Cloedboriogd which had control of Angelina is completely independent of *real* Cloedboriogd's presence, and *was* the real Cloedboriogd you met in India. Or the major part of his soul, anyway.'

'Oh. And the Articles Of Power…?'

'So, after you disappeared from Cloedboriogd's hideout, both the AOPs were left with him. There was no sign of yours, until you appeared here.'

'But we still don't know whether he found them or not…' Alex said doubtfully.

Vishwaroopaha sat thinking for a few moments, then spoke up. 'I get it now. Alex, your selfless choice was somehow related to the other choice. The Lost cabin did not command Fate to do opposite of what you had chosen, but the consequences of your choice were such that Cloedboriogd would be in a favorable position. You do not know how The Lost Cabin works. In the lost and forbidden Sternindian books, it is written that it only helps the user escape the danger in which he is. So, you disappeared from the spot, because The Lost Cabin knew you were endangered where you were, but the AOPs did not disappear with you, because only you had chosen the choice, not the AOPs. As for the AOPs, in the scene it was shown that they were delivered to you in your hands, but not where you were, or whether they will disappear with you or not.'

Alex took a moment to take it in. This was far more complicated than he had thought. He went over what Vishwaroopaha had said again and again, and Vishwaroopaha generously gave him time to comprehend before continuing.

'Your friends had to be saved in the other scene, but the scene did not say that they will surely be killed if you do not make that choice. Your friends surely felt like they were dying, but they did not. I don't know whether any of the two choices satisfied the situation of what you wanted to happen or not, in any way. I guess that you had to choose the opposite in order for things to happen the way you wanted them to. But, this also is not foolproof, because by making the other choice, I'm not sure whether you would have prevented Cloedboriogd from having both the AOPs and whether your friends would be saved. So, all in all, it seems like there is a fifty-fifty chance that Cloedboriogd has the AOPs, because they are not with you, and according to the scene which you had chosen, they are not with Cloedboriogd.'

'So… Have we failed?' Alex said.

No one replied. They all just stayed there, thinking.

An "ahem" from behind caught everyone's attention. It was Mentor Chakravarty. 'Since you all know what was at stake and were actively involved in the events that led to the incoming of the news I'm about to break, I think it's safe for you to know what I'm here to tell our principal,' he said.

'And what is that?' Vishwaroopaha asked, raising an eyebrow.

'Well, to keep it short and simple, I'd like to say–...'

Cloedboriogd has risen.